The chance to become involved in painting and constructing scenery for some of the major theatrical productions of the day was an opportunity too good for an ambitious young artist to miss, so at the tender age of sixteen, Ken Holdsworth quit art school for the bright lights of London's West End.

Two years later the National Service Act put him in uniform. This was the time of the Cold War, the Iron Curtain and the Berlin Wall, and he found himself in the Royal Air Force policing a divided Germany.

Returning to the world of art he became a structural and graphic designer of packaging, mainly for the cosmetic industries, where many of his original creations are still in everyday use.

POSSESSED

It is 1752 and His Britannic Majesty's sixty-gun ship-of the-line, *Indefatigable*, drops anchor at Fort St George, Madras, a trading post of the British East India Company ... Discover why Thomas Neville, an officer in the 22nd Regiment of Foot and heir to a title and estates back in England, serves on board as a common deckhand ... Follow his adventures in India, his friendship with the Empire builder, Robert Clive, his clash with the agents of Suraja Dowla, the sadistic Nawab of Bengal ... and back in England, his struggle against the sinister devil worshipper, the Reverend Edwin Cruikshank ...

Books by Ken Holdsworth
Published by The House of Ulverscroft:

THE FINAL CURTAIN

KEN HOLDSWORTH

POSSESSED

Complete and Unabridged

ULVERSCROFT
Leicester

First published in Great Britain in 2008 by
Willow
an imprint of Willow Bank Publishers Limited
Cambridgeshire

First Large Print Edition
published 2010
by arrangement with
Willow Bank Publishers Limited
Cambridgeshire

British Library CIP Data

Holdsworth, Ken.
Possessed.
1. Great Britain. Army. Regiment of Foot, 22nd- -
Officers- -Fiction. 2. Heirs- -England- -Fiction.
3. Great Britain- -History- -George II, *1727 – 1760-* -
Fiction. 4. India- -History- -18th century- -Fiction.
5. Clive, Robert Clive, Baron, *1725 – 1774-* -Fiction.
6. Adventure stories. 7. Large type books.
I. Title
823.9'2–dc22

ISBN 978–1–44480–211–5

Published by
F. A. Thorpe (Publishing)
Anstey, Leicestershire

Set by Words & Graphics Ltd.
Anstey, Leicestershire
Printed and bound in Great Britain by
T. J. International Ltd., Padstow, Cornwall

This book is printed on acid-free paper

To Ruby, my own precious gem, for without her unfailing support and encouragement this book would never have been written.

1

Madras, India, 1752

The sudden, sharp blow to the side of my head knocked me sideways. I grabbed the rail to stop myself falling. There was a roaring in my ear and something warm trickled down my face to drip off my chin. I wiped it away, instinctively looking at my hand as I did so; it was blood. Tentatively I felt my ear. It was still there but it was numb, the pain would come later.

'I'll make a sailor of you yet, Neville,' the bo'sun shouted. 'Get back to your work.'

Of all the impressed men on His Britannic Majesty's sixty-gun, ship-of-the-line, *Indefatigable*, he seemed to take a sadistic delight in singling me out for all the dirty jobs, and I'd taken just about as much as I could.

After months of having a rolling deck under my feet I longed with every fibre of my being to tread firm ground again so, at the shout of 'Land ho!' I had run to the rail and there it was, a dark ribbon stretching along the horizon as far as the eye could see. Excitedly, I called to Owen to come and look.

'I don't need to, boy,' he said. 'I can smell it. It's India.'

Owen had served in His Majesty's navy for years so I didn't doubt he'd been to this part of the globe before but as for him being able to tell a country by its smell, well, I wasn't so sure about that — but I took a good deep sniff anyway. What would it be, I wondered, this smell of India, the fragrance of exotic flowers on the warm offshore breeze or perhaps a heady aroma of rare spices?

Try as I might I couldn't detect anything beyond the salty tang of the sea and the smell of the skinned and gutted seabirds that cookie had pegged out to dry in the rigging.

And that was how the bo'sun found us; Owen on his knees conscientiously scrubbing away and me leaning on my mop, eyes closed and inhaling deeply.

The big Welshman helped me to my feet and stuck the mop back in my hand. 'Easy lad,' he muttered. 'Don't make it worse for yourself.'

I never did say anything to him about not being able to smell anything unusual. I wouldn't hurt his feelings for the world, which was funny in a way because he had been a member of the press-gang who dragged me aboard in the first place. And it had been Owen's big hand that had gripped my arm, stopping me from taking a swing at the bo'sun on my first terrible day at sea.

'That was just a taste of the rope's end for speaking out of turn, boy,' he whispered. 'Disobey a ship's officer and you gets a flogging, strike one and you'll be hanged.'

$$\star \quad \star \quad \star$$

I had awakened that morning with a splitting headache and the feeling that the floor I was lying on was moving. Gradually, I became aware of the noise of timbers creaking and that somewhere far away a fiddle was playing and men were singing. Then I heard a muffled voice shouting orders and the sound of running feet on the wooden planking above my head. Desperately, I racked my fuddled brain for some clue as to where I was and all I got were flashes of a noisy waterside tavern, the appearance of a young midshipman with a gang of tough looking sailors and a confused scramble with lots of screaming and shouting. I remember fending off grasping hands and yelling, 'You can't take me, I'm a gentleman!'

That was when the back of my head exploded and I blacked out.

I gingerly explored the tender spot with my fingertips. There was a lump that felt the size of a plovers egg and around it my hair was hard and matted with what I assumed to be dried blood. Then someone next to me vomited noisily.

I was soon to find out that there were eight of us crammed in the brig and once the ship was underway we were brought up on deck for the captain's inspection.

'God save me!' he said, making a show of disapproval. 'Where on earth did you find this motley collection of layabouts, Master Ellis?'

The young midshipman looked straight ahead. 'They were the best of a bad lot, sir,' he replied. 'Eight able-bodied men, as ordered.'

I stepped forward. 'Look here . . . '

'Get back in line,' growled someone from behind.

'I demand to be put ashore immediately,' I continued.

A mighty blow on my back brought me to my knees and my protestations to an end. As I scrambled to my feet I looked round and saw a thickset, brutish looking man wielding a short length of thick rope knotted at one end. I am no novice when it comes to bare knuckle boxing and I took a stance with fists clenched. It was then that Owen intervened.

After that incident the big Welshman took to watching over me with a fatherly eye, going

4

out of his way to show me the ropes and generally keeping me out of trouble. His stolid nature belied the fact that he was a reasonably well-educated man and a veritable mine of information about everything — except about his past and how he came to be in the navy. In all the time we spent together all I managed to glean from him was that he had once been a clerk at a slate quarry. It was my guess it had something to do with drink for I never saw him take his grog.

As weeks became months, one by one, my fellow pressed-men gave in and accepted their fate but I never lost a feeling of anger and resentment. I took more beatings and without Owen's restraining influence I would have incurred harsher punishments. He helped me through some of the blackest days of my life — so I would never deliberately hurt his feelings.

★　★　★

The shoreline was getting nearer and beyond a forest of masts in the harbour I could see what appeared to be fine houses and a church with a tall spire within a fortified wall. On one side of this enclave there was a colourful collection of more modest dwellings and to the other was what looked like the ruins of a

5

former settlement. I asked Owen if he knew the name of this place.

'Madras, boy. That's Fort St George dead ahead.'

I felt a rush of hope. 'It's got to be English with a name like that. Is it the army?'

'You're correct in the first part, boy. It's English right enough but it's not the army. That's an East India Company trading post that is. There is a small garrison of Company militia but they're a poor lot. Not like the Frenchies at Pondicherry, they've got proper soldiers.'

'Pondicherry?'

'That's a town about three-quarters of the way down the coast between here and Fort St David. That's another English post although, as it's named after the patron saint of Wales, I shouldn't be calling it English now should I?' He chuckled at his little joke. A mad thought had entered my head. Why don't I jump ship? The biggest deterrent to would-be abscond-ers, greater even than the fear of the flogging they would get if they were caught, was the thought of being alone in a foreign country with no money and no friends — but I knew someone who had gone to work in Madras! An old school chum, a rough-hewn country lad and a bit of a rebel as I recall. I felt sure he would enjoy helping me to put one over on

His Majesty's navy.

The guns of the fort boomed a welcome as we sailed into the harbour, our wake causing a flotilla of small fishing boats to rock and sway as we passed them. Getting away from the ship proved to be easy. A work party was to be sent ashore to provision *Indefatigable* with fresh fruit, so all I had to do was to be where the bo'sun could see me and sure enough I was picked to go along.

We were anchored a little way offshore, alongside a portly East Indiaman, so my group had to clamber down the scramble net to some flat-bottomed boats, which then set off for the colourful sprawl of shanties to the right of the fort. This, as I was to learn later, was the Indian town, a place of bustle and noise, and a pungent smell, a putrid mixture of garlic, rancid coconut oil and stagnant ditches. I thought of Owen's 'smell of India' and I smiled.

A great mountain of fruit had already been delivered to the water's edge and while everyone from the ship was busy filling baskets and hefting them on their shoulders to take back to the boats I slipped into the crowd without anyone noticing. With my immediate objective being to put as much distance between the shore party and myself as quickly as possible, I thrust my way through the milling throng in the street and dodged out of sight behind some mud huts.

The sound of raised voices and what seemed to me like the cry of someone in pain caused me to wheel around and I saw several natives grouped around something in the shadows that looked, at first, like a bundle of old clothes. They were all shouting and kicking at the object which, on closer inspection, turned out to be a small man curled up into a ball, his thin arms wrapped around his bald head in a vain attempt to protect himself from the vicious blows of his assailants.

Before joining the working party I had filched a wooden belaying pin from the rack and stuck it in the waistband of my trousers. I drew it out and with a shout I waded in.

There were three of them kicking the man in the road. One was doing most of the shouting, whether he was urging the other two on or just screaming abuse at the bloody bundle in the road I neither knew nor cared. I felled him easily with a blow to the back of his skull and grabbed one of the others by the scruff of his neck. I whacked this fellow across the back of his legs with my belaying pin and he dropped to his knees, a sharp tap on the head left him lying across the body of his associate. The third ruffian came at me with a knife. I kicked him hard, just below the knee, and as he went down I slashed upwards with my cudgel. The blow caught him across the jaw, flinging back his head with a loud snap.

The small man sat up and began fussing with his garment, which was nothing more than a large piece of saffron-coloured cloth. He drew it around his scrawny body with great care, attempting to brush off the dirt and bloodstains with a claw-like hand.

As I helped him to his feet, he said, 'I would know your name, *sahib.*'

He was of a great age with yellowy-brown skin stretched tightly across his face, emphasising his cheekbones. His eyes were as black as boot-buttons and there was so much intimacy in his gaze that I felt uncomfortable and had to look away.

'Tom Neville,' I replied. It took a moment before I realised that this little native had spoken to me in my own language.

'Hari Lal thanks you, Tom Neville,' he said. 'Those followers of *Kali* would have taken my life. I am forever in your debt.'

I sensed someone behind me and I wheeled around with my belaying pin at the ready. I did not expect to see English soldiers.

'Your first time in India, sailor, am I right?'

The soldier addressing me was a big man

with a round, shiny-red face, deeply furrowed down one side by a badly healed sword cut that drew the corner of his mouth up in a permanent leer. He carried a musket and looked uncomfortably hot in his uniform, which was a faded scarlet coat, buttoned white leggings, a badly stained white waistcoat and a dusty, black, tricorne hat. There was another soldier with him similarly attired but of much smaller stature. He had positioned himself a few feet away with his back to us porting his weapon defensively. In spite of their disreputable appearance these soldiers represented the local authority so it was with some trepidation that I replied it was my first visit to this country.

'I thought as much,' he said.

He moved closer, so close I could see the sweat trickling down his pockmarked cheeks and soaking into the grubby and poorly tied stock at his neck. I tried to ignore his smell, which was an evil mixture of stale sweat and cheap gin.

'Listen lad,' he whispered. 'I've got a bit of advice for you. Next time you sees a bit of a ruckus, unless it's a white man what's being set on, you let 'em get on with it. You was lucky that bloke you rescued didn't knife you when your back was turned. Murdering bastards they are, the lot of them.'

Suddenly remembering Hari Lal, I turned to look for him but he had vanished.

The soldier eyed me suspiciously. ''Ere, what are you doing wandering around Black Town on your own anyway?'

'I'm looking for the East India Company,' I said.

He laughed and called to his companion. 'Hear that Archie? Jolly Jack Tar 'ere is looking for the East India Company.'

The other man, still with his back to us, shouted back, 'A bit off course, aint he?'

'What would you be wanting with the Company then?' Scarface asked, smiling at me, quizzically.

'I'm looking for an old school friend of mine. He came to Madras to work for them as a writer, a clerk, but last I heard he'd transferred to their military.'

'Did he now — and what might his name be then?'

'Robert Clive.'

The soldier's face lost its smile. A nervous tic twitched the scarred side of his face and he grabbed the front of my shirt. 'Are you trying to be funny!' he shouted.

The soldier called Archie stepped between us laying a restraining hand on his comrade's arm, 'Steady on, Dan. I'm sure he meant no disrespect.' He was a little cockney sparrow of a man with small dark eyes, a sharp pointed nose and a receding chin. He reminded me of a ferret I had once owned.

Scarface grudgingly released his grip and I stuffed my shirtfront back into my trousers.

'Don't mind him,' the small man said with a conciliatory smile. 'Robert Clive's a hero to every soldier out here, but to Dan he's more than that. Dan was with him at Arcot you see.'

I didn't know where Arcot was and at that precise moment I didn't care. I was still smarting from his companion's sudden outburst. Had it not been for ferret-face's quick intervention his ugly partner would have been on the receiving end of the belaying pin that I still held in my hand — and God knows where that would have led!

'Captain Clive was a Company clerk,' Archie continued, 'but when the French took Fort St George . . . '

Dan spat contemptuously. 'The garrison here then was bloody useless,' he said, producing a silver hipflask from his coat pocket and unscrewing the cap. 'A bunch of drunks they was, the lot of them.' He put the flask to his lips and disposed of its contents in a few noisy gulps.

Ferret-face nodded in agreement. 'When

the French took Fort St George,' he repeated, 'Robert Clive disguised himself as a native and made his way south through French territory to Fort St David — that's another British post some fifty miles away — and there he joined the Company's army.'

'There's only one Robert Clive,' Dan said, his eyes shining with pride. 'The Frogs at St George handed the fort back after they'd looted it and burnt it down. The fat English merchants pretended everything was all right again but us soldiers knew they wouldn't stop there . . . '

Archie took up the story. 'It was obvious to anyone who didn't have his head up his arse that Fort St David would be their next target. Company soldiers were a bloody joke to the French and with good reason. Clive said what we needed was a victory, something to make the French think twice about taking us on, so he talks the governor into making him an unpaid captain and takes as many men as could be spared from the garrison and goes and captures Arcot.'

'With just two hundred men, and most of them half-trained native *sepoys*,' Dan said proudly. 'We took on a combined French and Indian army of over fifteen thousand. And they had bloody great battle-elephants as well! We hadn't come up against anything like that before and didn't know how to deal with them but Captain Clive tells our gunners to shoot at their flanks which made the poor wounded beasts run amok, killing more of their soldiers than we could ever hope to.' His ugly face twisted with a broad grin as he relived that grisly episode. Becoming serious again and in a voice that was almost a whisper, he said, solemnly, 'One night they puts up this almighty barrage. We all thought our time was up — and so did the captain because he told us to stand firm and sell our lives dearly — but the assault never came. When the sun came up they'd all packed up and gone.'

Dan stood there smiling and little Archie leapt in to carry on with the story. 'When Clive left Arcot, he met up with the enemy again about twenty miles south,' he said excitedly. 'And even though he was still outnumbered he gave them another good drubbing. That made some of those pro-French Indian princes think again, I can tell you. Natives flocked to join Clive's little army, so many that he had to turn a lot of them away because he didn't have the weapons for them. Not bad for a lad still in his twenties, eh?'

The two garrulous soldiers walked me back to their barracks in Fort St George, talking all the way. 'You should find Captain Clive at his house in Charles Street,' Archie said when we got there. 'He's gone back to his old job of being the fort's steward and commissary.'

Dan sniffed. 'And why shouldn't he take it easy for a bit? He's had nothing else but sieges and battles for two bloody years! He's not one of your namby-pamby officers who keeps well out of the enemy's range either. The captain was always in the thick of things with men being shot down all round him.'

I finally managed to extricate myself from their company by promising to mention how helpful they had been when I met up with my old schoolmate.

'You be sure to tell the captain we're ready to march with him again when he gives the word,' Dan shouted as I walked away.

I wondered what I'd let myself in for. I'd set out to meet a humble clerk for God's sake, not a military legend!

★ ★ ★

I found the street without difficulty; the buildings in it were large and airy with shutters to shield them from the fierce sun. On a corner, in a patch of shade, a small group of Europeans were talking. One of them, a thin, elegantly dressed man with a long, silver topped cane, saw me coming. He eyed me up and down as if I was something he'd just scraped from the sole of his shoe. I was aware of my sweat-stained shirt and soiled sailcloth trousers but ignoring his disdainful look I went straight to them.

'Excuse me, gentlemen,' I said politely, touching the brim of my straw hat in the approved manner. 'Would you be so kind as to tell me which is Robert Clive's house?'

'Good heavens!' the tall man said. 'The ruffian is asking for the steward.'

'Perhaps he carries a message from the man-o'-war in the harbour,' suggested a young man with dark, Levantine looks. He flashed me a smile, which I was happy to return.

'Nonsense, Tobias,' another said, dabbing at his fleshy face with a large white handkerchief. He was somewhat older than the others and judging by his florid complexion he hadn't been in India long. 'The Royal Navy wouldn't dare send Robert Clive a messenger below midshipman rank.' He turned and flapped the damp handkerchief at me dismissively. 'Go back to your ship, fellow, and sort your problems out with your superior.'

I stood my ground. 'I'm sure he would make time for me.'

'Damned impudence!' the first man shouted. 'Be gone, or I'll call a guard and have you flogged.'

'Watch out,' the older man whispered. 'He's here.'

I turned and saw a tall man dressed in an expensive-looking beige coat, ruffed shirt and white silk breeches approaching us. The heavy brow, large nose and the sensitive yet determined mouth were all a little older but there was no doubt that this was the rebellious youth I remembered so well. Before anyone could stop me I stepped forward.

'Robert!' I shouted. 'It's me, Tom Neville. I was in your class at Doctor Eaton's school in Allostock.'

Someone grabbed my arm. The dignitary stopped, raised a curious eyebrow and held up a hand.

'Release him,' he said.

He was instantly obeyed. I snatched off my hat and he peered into my face.

'My dear Neville,' he said.

There was an audible sigh of relief from all around. He held out his hand and I grasped it willingly. He didn't know me from Adam; it was there in his eyes. But this was a true English gentleman and for that I was very grateful.

Much to the chagrin of the little group he sent them away and instead invited me into the small mansion that was his home. He motioned me to wait in the lofty entrance hall whilst he disappeared into its interior. I stood with my hat in my hands for what seemed like an age. Granted, it was cooler waiting there than it would have been outside in the hot afternoon sun but the thought that perhaps I had been forgotten began to niggle.

I was pondering my next move when a voice behind me boomed: 'Master Neville, I'm sorry you have been kept waiting.' The heels of Clive's buckled shoes rapped across the marble floor as he strode towards me. 'Now then, sir, what is it I can do for you?'

He was in his shirtsleeves, his linen snow-white against his deeply tanned skin.

'You didn't remember me, did you, sir?'

Clive smiled. 'Was it that obvious? I'm sorry, but I didn't stay at Doctor Eaton's school very long and it wasn't exactly yesterday, don't y'know.'

I tried a new tack. 'Do you recall an evening when a group of us students slipped out of school to visit the fair on Knutsford Heath . . . and we got into a fight with some gypsy lads.'

'Yes I do!' he said slowly and a faraway look came into his eyes as if he were savouring the memory. 'When the good doctor refused us permission to go, I said we should climb out of the dormitory window . . . and I remember that fight!' His face lit up with pleasure. 'All the other lads ran away and left just me and one other boy to face those ruffians.' He suddenly roared with laughter. 'You're going to tell me you were that other boy?'

I nodded.

Still chuckling he led me to a drawing room. Like the hall, it was spacious with a high ceiling and a marble floor. Huge mirrors adorned the walls and the impression was one of elegance rather than an excess of decoration. Waving me toward a long upholstered seat littered with silk cushions, he made his way to a beautifully inlaid low marble table in the centre of the room and proceeded to fill two silver goblets from a bell-shaped decanter. Conscious of my dirty trousers I could not bring myself to sit on his fine upholstery.

Clive came over with the goblets. 'I'm sorry Neville,' he said, 'but people change. You must agree you are no longer that skinny little boy who so courageously stood back to back with me in that scuffle on Knutsford Heath.'

I took the cup he held out to me and sipped its contents. It was Madeira, the first I had tasted since leaving home. It was nectar. I was very thirsty and forgetting my manners I emptied the goblet. Clive smiled understandingly and took it away for a refill.

'Neville,' he muttered to himself. 'Neville, Neville, Neville.' Suddenly, he turned, his brown face beaming and he wagged a knowing finger. 'I've got you! Your father is Sir Rupert Neville, the magistrate, am I right?'

'Yes, Sir Rupert is my father, but he quit the bench following a particularly unpleasant experience.'

Clive was busily pouring more wine. 'Really?' he said. 'And what was that, pray?'

It occurred to me later that this question was possibly asked only out of politeness, but my father's account of the experience that led to his resignation was etched deep in my mind and, being relaxed a little by the Madeira, I found myself relating it in detail.

★ ★ ★

When he arrived at Knutsford prison it was still dark, but even without being able to see the grim structure, he knew that the gallows would be there in the prison yard just as he knew it would be dismantled immediately after today's proceedings. It was customary

20

for the condemned man to be hanged at dawn, and one of the least enviable duties of a magistrate, is to be present and witness due execution of the court's verdict.

It had been a cold ride and he was grateful to the prison governor for the large brandy he had waiting for him in his chambers.

'This one will be no trouble, Your Honour,' he said. 'I've never seen a man about to be hung so cocky and self-assured.'

'I have always been most envious of self-assurance, most envious indeed.'

The speaker was a pale young cleric with delicate features and the ethereal look of a person not long for this world. He stood with shoulders bent and hands clasped meekly before his chest in an attitude of apologetic humility.

The governor led my father away from him explaining that the prison chaplain, the Reverend Doctor Norris, was indisposed and this was the new curate from the parish church who, at the last moment, had been instructed to deputise for him. He shook his head sadly.

'This is his first execution,' he said, tut-tutting. 'And the poor fellow is facing an early grave himself.' He looked across at the young man pityingly and whispered, 'He'll not make old bones, he has consumption.'

The young priest was still talking to whoever cared to listen. 'Many's the time,' he said, 'That I have marvelled how some people can enter a room without saying a word and be afforded immediate attention, whereas others are completely ignored.'

'I know the feeling,' the governor replied, forcing a laugh, 'I always seem to be in a blind spot whenever I try to get served in a crowded tavern.'

The first grey light of dawn was beginning to show in the sky and he indicated it was time to go. He led them outside to where the scaffold stood grim and businesslike in the cobbled courtyard. The hangman was kneeling down in front of the prisoner, busily lashing his ankles together, his wrists having been tied in his cell before he was brought out. My father remembered that the condemned man had appeared tall in the dock, but silhouetted against the morning sky he looked a giant, his hair hanging loose in long, twisted tendrils that moved Medusa-like in the chilly breeze. The felon followed the governor's party with wild, staring eyes. He sought out my father and having made eye contact, held him with a look of ferocious intensity. He called down to him. 'I'm pleased you're the witnessing magistrate at my execution, Your Honour, as it is you I have to thank for being here this fine morning.'

My father tore his eyes from his hypnotic look, telling himself that this man had been tried and convicted of murder by due process of law. Why should he feel any guilt!

The man continued to speak. 'Mark this day well, Sir Rupert Neville. For today there is both a beginning and an ending. For me, this is an end and for you, Your Honour, it is a beginning.' He paused, and with a voice dripping with venom, added, 'The end of a chapter in my life and the beginning of the end for you and your line!'

My father had received many threats to his life, both from the dock and from the gallows, but this was said with such cold determination that it really unnerved him.

The young cleric climbed the scaffold and, holding the Bible out in front of him like a shield, he delivered what was required of him. 'You have broken God's Holy Law and Commandments,' he said, his small voice trembling with fear. 'Repent now or you will not go to Heaven!'

My father says he will never, ever, forget what happened next.

'What do I want with your Heaven?' the condemned man replied, and at that moment, a black cloud blotted out the sun and the rope binding the prisoner's wrists miraculously fell away. Throwing his arms wide, he cried out, 'My master is the Prince of *this* world. He has only one law. DO WHAT YOU WILL!'

The governor frantically signalled to the hangman who released the catch holding the trap. As the prisoner fell, he grabbed hold of the young curate and the two men went down into the void together, the additional weight on the rope audibly snapping the prisoner's neck.

When the young priest was disentangled from this macabre embrace he did a strange and unexpected thing, he laughed.

★ ★ ★

'Good Lord!' Clive exclaimed. 'The shock must have sent the poor fellow off his head.'

'Quite so. They say his hair turned white overnight.'

My host insisted that I stay and dine with him and placed me in the hands of his *dubash*, his valet. I followed this taciturn Indian to one of the guest bedrooms where, indicating that I should wait, he left me. I hardly had time to explore my new surroundings before he returned accompanied by a whole retinue of servants carrying a hipbath, several huge jugs of steaming hot water, a stack of towels and some soap. There was also a razor. I made a face at the wild man in the mirror and with some scissors I found on the dressing table, set to work trimming my beard as short as I could.

I was shaving my chin in the luxury of my first hot bath for months when to my complete surprise and utter delight the valet reappeared with an outfit of clothes for me including shoes and a rather splendid brown velvet coat.

I couldn't remember the last time I felt this clean — or smelled as wholesome. I dressed in my new finery, enjoying again the sensuous feel of silk against my skin and the crisp, fresh-air smell of clean linen. I looked back in the mirror and got quite a shock to see someone I had almost forgotten returning my gaze.

The familiar sound of a dinner-gong brought me out of my trance and after dragging a comb quickly through my hair and pulling on the velvet coat, I made my way down the elegant staircase, at the bottom of which I was met by a servant and escorted to a candle-lit dining room where I found my host dressed in the full regalia of an Indian prince. He was talking to the young Jewish merchant that I had seen with the other Europeans in Charles Street that afternoon.

He waved away my look of surprise with; 'European garments are not suited to this climate . . . Come, Neville, sit yourself down. There's only the three of us dining tonight. You've met Toby Bloom, of course.'

I nodded to my fellow dinner guest who smiled back at me. He was a darkly handsome man whose face showed great strength of character and eyes that had an intelligent, honest, straight-dealing look about them. There are some people I take an instant liking to, Tobias Bloom was one of them.

'Toby's family have been merchants in the City of London for over two hundred years,' Clive went on. 'They have contacts everywhere, which has proved invaluable to me in the job I do here.'

He seemed more relaxed than before, but for the first time I noticed how very tired he looked. I attempted to thank him for his overwhelming hospitality but he motioned me to silence.

'It would be a poor world where one cannot be generous to a friend,' he said.

By way of conversation, I asked if he was planning a new campaign.

He leaned back in the ornate gilded carver while the wine was poured. 'I've had my bellyful of battles. My job as the fort's steward and commissary has been left to others for long enough, it's time I took up the reins again.'

He tasted the wine and nodded his approval to the servant; the man then proceeded to fill the other glasses. 'God damn it, Neville,' he said. 'There have been too many occasions when those standing at my side have been struck down. How long can a person go on cheating death, eh?'

He sat brooding for a moment, sipping his wine and surveying me quizzically. 'But what of you?' he said at length, 'Your father owns the best part of Cheshire. What the devil are you doing half way round the world dressed as a common seaman, eh? Come on, old Neville, tell all. You can speak feely in front of Toby here.'

What the devil indeed. Clive's turn of phrase, although unintentional, was chillingly accurate. I drank deeply from my glass and began my story.

2

Cheshire, England. Some six months earlier.

It is only when you no longer have something that you realise its value.

There was a time when I would wake up in the morning and look forward to each new day. I suppose that was happiness, but I never consciously thought about it.

I was young and fit, the heir to a large country estate, a captain in the British Army — and head over heels in love. I had everything and I wanted for nothing.

That is until the day Edwin Cruikshank came into my life.

★ ★ ★

It was beginning to get dark when I rode into Josh Napper's Farm. I'd chosen his place as my last call of the day for many reasons, one of them being that his farmhouse doubled as the only tavern in the tiny hamlet of Goostrey and I was more than ready for a tankard or two of Josh's finest ale. It was on my way home and I'd been about as far as you could expect to get in one day, if you were calling on every farm in the area.

Rent was collected from the tenants four times a year and as I was on leave from my regiment, my father had talked me into performing the task for this, the Michaelmas quarter.

'I know the bailiff is quite capable of doing the job, Thomas,' he said as he sent me off. 'But it's good for someone from the family to get out and meet the tenants occasionally and see how they're managing their properties. Being a landowner is a sacred trust, my boy. I'm as much a royalist as the next man, but to me the Neville estate is a Commonwealth and I am its Lord Protector. I make the rules here, and I say that the land is for the good of all who live and work on it — provided they look after it.'

The ring of my horse's hooves on the wet cobbles brought old Simon, Josh's ostler, hurrying out to hold the bridle while I dismounted. Another reason for staying over at Josh's tavern was that I was loath to cross the heath at this time of day carrying so much money. I said as much to Simon as I heaved the weighty saddlebags off my horse's steaming flanks. There was much talk of inns and taverns being in league with highway-men, but I had known Josh all my life and I trusted him and his people implicitly.

Simon was the very antithesis of his master. Where Josh was fat and jolly, he was thin and grumpy. He was also very talkative which I put down to him only having a row of horse's backsides for company for the greater part of the day.

'The heath's a lot safer now that terrible sinner, Black Jack Belcher, has gone to his final judgement,' he said, leading my horse away. 'While his corpse hung in the gibbet at the crossroads there wasn't anyone robbed hereabouts. It was there for two month, you must have seen it. The vicar had them take it down when someone stole the head.'

I was horrified. 'Who would do a thing like that?'

Simon stopped, looked about him and said in hushed whisper, 'There's some folk who reckons it were Welsh Meg, may the good Lord forgive her. They says she uses Black Jack's skull as her mixing bowl.'

Megan Griffith, or Welsh Meg as she was more commonly known, was notorious in Goostrey. Tall and wild looking, with a great mane of flyaway hair as black as a raven's wing, she lived in a ruin of a cottage on the outskirts of the village. Children would throw stones at her door and mothers snatched their babies off the street when they saw her coming. Some called her a witch — but never to her face. Although she was ostracized by the good people of the village and vilified from the pulpit of St Luke's, there was never a shortage of young maidens who secretly visited her cottage for her love potions. And many a farmer I knew had bottles filled with a decoction of hers buried at the corners of his fields to ward off the cowpox.

The word was that she sold other favours, more physical than mystical, but I wouldn't know about that, although she *was* a handsome woman.

'They do say she does a sure remedy for the brewer's droop,' Simon was saying, 'but you won't catch me swallowing no stinkhorn poached in maiden's water, 'specially if it's stirred up in Jack Belcher's brainbox.'

The thought of it made my flesh creep. What I needed was the welcoming, smoky warmth of the taproom, so I left Simon to his horses — and his gruesome thoughts — and crossed the yard to the tavern door. I couldn't think of anything nicer at that moment than to be sitting with my boots off, toasting my toes in front of a warm fire, and a tankard of Josh's ale in my hand.

I shouldered the door open. Inside, it was unusually noisy and so crowded I could barely see the fireplace, let alone a chair to sit in.

Josh was there, in the midst of all the commotion, with both arms high above his head, a clutch of foaming tankards in each hand. He was uncommonly corpulent for a farmer and getting through the crush was obviously not easy for him but he looked happy enough and traded good-natured banter with his customers as he squeezed between them. The sound of the door slamming behind me stopped him in his tracks and he peered through the fug to see who had just come in. He saw me and nodded his head as a greeting.

'Be with you in a jiffy, Master Thomas,' he shouted over the hubbub.

A man of about my own age dressed all in black stood with one booted foot on the stone hearth of the big inglenook fireplace. He was holding court before a group of slack-jawed locals who hung on his every word, occasionally bursting into loud raucous laughter. He glanced across and for a brief moment our eyes met. There was something odd about those eyes that I couldn't put my finger on but whatever it was it didn't mar his good looks. The man was nauseatingly handsome with a straight nose over lips almost feminine in their sensuality. He reminded me of the satyr in that huge painting in the long gallery at home — the one I had always run past as a child.

Having successfully delivered the order Josh came over to me, wiping his hands on his apron, a huge grin on his round, podgy face.

'All it takes is one gentleman to start buying drinks all round and the word spreads through the village like wildfire,' he said happily, nodding in the direction of the man in black.

I looked instead beyond the handsome stranger to where Josh's daughter was busily filling more pots from a large pewter jug. He didn't know it but she was another reason why I chose to spend the night here instead of riding those extra few miles home.

Emily had arrived in Goostrey with her father when she was just a baby. He had come at my father's invitation, one of his 'good works'. The farm needed a new tenant and Master Napper needed employment. There was no Mistress Napper. It was generally understood she had died in childbirth. Josh never spoke about his past but he must have had innkeeping somewhere in his background because it wasn't long before he had turned the farmhouse into a tavern, with my father's blessing, of course, and a most popular place it had soon become.

Emily blossomed into a fine-looking girl with coffee coloured skin and big brown eyes. I found myself greatly attracted to her and when I came home on leave I would find excuses to go into the village to look for her. We would exchange a smile or perhaps make a little polite conversation but nothing more. That is until the last time I called at her father's tavern.

It had been a long, tiring ride from Chester and I was glad to break my journey at Josh's farm. Old Simon was nowhere to be found and I was leading my horse into the stable when I heard the sound of running feet behind me. It was Emily.

'Oh, Thomas, it's you,' she said, breathlessly. 'Simon's not at work today, so I'm tending to the horses.'

She smiled at me and I was struck by how lovely she looked in the lamplight.

'Is there anything you don't do around here?' I asked.

'My father won't let me brew ale,' she said seriously, and then she laughed.

I laughed too. It felt good just to be with her. Then I did something I had wanted to do for a long time, I kissed her. To my delight she responded eagerly. She was soft and warm with a friendly puppy-dog smell, so

34

unlike the stiff and starchy, lavender-scented young ladies I was expected to partner at the hunt ball. I was transported to heaven, but then, quite unexpectedly, she pushed me away.

'Dear, sweet Tom,' she whispered. 'This will never do. We live in different worlds you and I. To let our feelings run away with us it will only bring heartache.'

I looked into her honest brown face and knew I was hopelessly in love with her.

* * *

Josh's voice brought me back to the present. 'We don't often get a real gentlemen staying here,' he mused, surveying the busy scene with obvious gratification. Then, suddenly realising to whom he was talking, hastily added, 'With the exception of yourself, of course, Master Thomas.' He beckoned to his daughter. 'My trade is mostly travellers you see, sir,' he said, covering his embarrassment by wiping the surface of a nearby table with the corner of his apron. 'Carters and drovers and the like . . . And they only get a room if they're clean! Hawkers and tinkers, they sleeps in the barn.' He spat on the floor. Emily arrived and bobbed a curtsey. 'Take Master Thomas to his room,' he said.

I looked for some sign from the girl, a surreptitious wink perhaps, or even the ghost of a smile, but there was nothing. She turned on her heel and without a word began threading her lissom body between the patrons of the smoky taproom. The girl moved with the grace of a dancer whilst I, in my caped, ankle-length, riding coat and carrying two heavy saddlebags, did my best not to leave too much chaos in my wake. I stopped briefly to apologise to a ruddy-faced countryman for causing him to spill ale down the front of his smock when another great roar of laughter went up from the fireside. It was plain that the stranger enjoyed being the centre of attention. There was an arrogant confidence about him that I found curiously fascinating. When I first saw him I had assumed that, in keeping with his clerical attire, he was wearing a wig but now that I was closer I could see that the long white hair he wore tied neatly at the back of his head with a large black bow was his own.

'Are you coming, sir?'

Emily had reached the stairs and I hastened to catch up with her. I was eager to get to my room. The master of the house always provided me with his best. I would have, as always, the large chamber on the first floor at the back of the house where it was quieter. There would be lots of hot water to wash away the dust and dirt of the journey, a fire burning merrily in the grate and a table set for supper. I was surprised, therefore, when Emily went right past the door and showed me instead into a small closet that smelled heavily of mildew and had no fireplace.

'If you will give me your coat, sir, I'll dry it for you,' she said.

I threw the saddlebags on the bed in disgust. I was angry and disappointed — and puzzled. Why was Emily being so formal? It had always been, 'Master Thomas' in the presence of her father, 'Thomas' when we were alone — and then on my last visit, when we kissed, it had been a whispered, 'Dear, sweet Tom.'

Taking the pistols from the pockets I gave her the coat. 'I suppose that gentleman downstairs has my usual room. Who is he, Emily?'

'His name is Cruikshank, sir ... The Reverend Edwin Cruikshank.' She spoke the name softly and for a long moment she stood clutching my wet coat to her bosom before she caught my eye and hurriedly became all-businesslike again. 'He's here to visit Welsh Meg ... He says he's her brother.'

That the haughty stranger downstairs

should be related to the village witch raised more questions in my mind than I was prepared to deal with at that moment. My main concern was what was wrong with Emily, so I took the plunge and asked her.

'Why, nothing, sir,' she said, avoiding eye contact. 'Now I really must go. We are very busy tonight and my father needs me downstairs.'

She used the same excuse again later when she came back with some ale and a plate of mutton stew.

I ate a miserable supper sitting on the edge of the lumpy bed. With the customers having gone home the inn was quiet. It was cold now that the sun had gone down so I decided to go to the kitchen and retrieve my coat. Damp it may be, but its weight would provide a welcome supplement to the thin blankets Josh had left on this bed.

I was also determined to have it out with his daughter once and for all.

Taking a candle I stepped into the corridor outside. As I did so, I caught a glimpse of Emily slipping into my old room. I had to pass the door and when I got there I hesitated. I wanted to know what was going on but I couldn't just barge in, could I? She was probably only bringing the reverend his supper or a clean towel, or something. A sudden cry from within decided my next move and without stopping to think I snapped open the latch and went inside. My flickering candle picked out the figure of Cruikshank lying on a dishevelled bed with Emily in his arms. The look on her face told me the cry I heard had not been one of pain, but of pleasure.

This was something that even in my worst nightmares I would never have conceived possible. Here was the person I loved, the sweet, innocent child who had drawn the line at a stolen kiss, proven before my eyes to be nothing more than a no-good wanton.

Consumed by anger I stormed back to my room, grabbed my belongings and went down to the kitchen. Josh was there but I said nothing about what I had just seen. He expressed both surprise and disappointment when I told him I was not staying but paid up willingly when I asked for his rent. I then snatched my coat and left.

★ ★ ★

A bright, frosty moon shone from a cloudless sky but I was in no mood to enjoy the beauty of the night. I spurred my tired horse on at a canter until we were well clear of the heath, allowing him to slow to a trot only when the tall, twisted chimneys of my home came into view.

Dunmere Hall is a timber-framed, moated manor house. For centuries the moat's only use was to keep out inquisitive cattle but it came into its own as a defence against stray bands of Scots looters on their way back north after the rebellion of '45.

My illustrious ancestor, Richard de Neville, built the original great hall three hundred years ago and since then each subsequent occupier has either added to it or altered it in some way, resulting in a rambling, picturesque, jumble of pointed gables and overhanging upper stories.

The clatter of my horse's hooves on the stone bridge over the moat brought out a sleepy footman and a motley collection of dogs that milled around my horse, playfully yapping and snapping at its legs. The imperturbable Sergeant Finch stood at the far end of the bridge and with him was my dog, Hagar. Finch snapped his fingers and Hagar leaped forward and in a few seconds had the other dogs rounded up and penned like sheep in the archway below the gatehouse.

Hagar is a lurcher, a poacher's dog, a cross between a retriever and a greyhound. I found her last winter wandering the lanes half-starved looking for her owner who was no doubt paying the price for his crimes in some lockup somewhere. I called her Hagar because it means 'the forsaken'. Regular meals and exercise plus a lot of loving care worked wonders and she is now a happy and healthy dog. She earns her keep by catching the rats in Finch's stables but when I'm home she chooses to stay close to me, and would have been with me on my quarter-day round had not an unexplained bout of sickness prevented her. I was greatly relieved to see she was over it.

Finch stepped forward and touched the brim of his hat. 'Welcome home, sir,' he said.

He is an old cavalryman and claims to be able to hear a rider approaching a mile off, which is probably true, for never have I arrived home without finding him waiting to relieve me of my mount. I dismounted and handed him my reins.

'Hagar seems to have got over whatever it was that upset her,' I said.

'She rallied as soon as you were gone, sir. Like there'd never been anything wrong with her.'

Finch led my horse away, and with Hagar at my heels, I followed the yawning footman through the entrance porch, across the courtyard and into the great hall.

This is a vast room with a high, arched

roof, oak panelled walls, tall bow windows, and a familiar and comforting smell, which is a blend of wood smoke from the big fireplace and the rush matting that covers the stone floor. A long refectory table on a raised dais filled one end of the room. This was only used when we were entertaining important guests, as my mother preferred the round table in the smaller and brighter parlour for family meals.

I instructed the man to leave my bags and dismissed him. He hurried away, no doubt eager to get back to his warm cot in the gatehouse. I was more than ready for bed myself and made my way wearily up the wide staircase. On reaching my room I crashed out on the bed fully dressed and slept soundly until dawn when Hagar, licking my face, awakened me. After a quick wash and a change of linen I was ready to go downstairs and greet the day.

Arriving at the parlour I found my father already sitting at the round table with a plate of his usual kidneys and sausage before him, and the small glass of brandy he regularly took with breakfast near to hand. He looked up and nodded, showing no sign of surprise, or even pleasure at seeing me. His appearance was quite formidable and I often wondered how the miscreants who had the misfortune to appear before him must have felt. Blue-grey eyes as cold as ice, a long, thin, aquiline nose above a mouth that was nothing more than a cruel, hard gash and iron-grey hair that he wore combed back severely from his high forehead. In the ten years since the death of my elder brother, I had grown used to my father being taciturn and uncommunicative. At first this worried me as I thought he was blaming me for Ned's death but as I grew older I came to realise it was just his way of handling his grief.

My parents had been blessed with three sons. Ned was their firstborn, followed two years later by me and then after a gap of eight years, Giles had arrived. Nothing very out of the ordinary in that you might say but, many years later, I was to discover that shortly after I was born my father was told that his wife would bear him no more children, so Giles must have come as a surprise.

To my mother, the new baby was nothing less than a miracle.

Sir Rupert had always been adamant that family tradition must be followed and the heir to the baronetcy should inherit the estate in its entirety. This left my younger brother and me with the only two career options open to younger sons of the gentry, the military and the church.

My future was revealed to me on my fourteenth birthday. With everyone assembled in the drawing room, my father solemnly announced that as I was approaching the end of my schooldays he was making arrangements to purchase a commission for me in our county regiment. This was what I had been hoping and praying for. I was so happy and excited that I almost wept with joy, which would not have been the wisest thing to do under the circumstances.

A few days later he took me to visit the twenty-second of foot at their depot in Chester. We dined in style as guests of the Officer's Mess and afterwards the colonel introduced me to his staff. Meeting the rough, tough sergeants and the very grand and slightly standoffish officers did nothing to diminish my desire to be one of their number, in fact it had quite the opposite effect. The colonel I had met before, as he was my uncle, my father's younger brother. With the papers signed, the die was cast and I came away from Chester barracks looking forward to the day when I too would be cutting a dash in the King's scarlet coat. What I did not know was that a terrible tragedy was about to befall the Neville family that would mean a delay to the start of my military career.

A few days after that visit, Ned and I were

skylarking and he slipped and fell down some slimy steps. Boys can be terribly cruel and unsympathetic, and I was no exception. At the time I thought it very funny to see my big brother take a tumble and I even teased him for being a coward when, days later, he was still complaining of pain and stiffness in his leg. Why was he making such a fuss? What was a skinned knee for goodness sake! What I didn't know was that the wound had become infected and by the time a physician was sent for it was too late. Ned died, and my childhood died with him.

⋆ ⋆ ⋆

'God bless you, sinner,' said a voice from over by the sideboard.

'Amen to that,' I replied.

The parlour is in the east wing and both of its outside walls are virtually all window. It is therefore invariably light early in the day, but on this particular morning it was dazzlingly bright with sunlight streaming in through the patterned glass. It wasn't until my eyes became properly adjusted that I could see there was someone else in the room. All I could make out was a man of medium height dressed in black.

It was not unusual to find a member of the

clergy at our table. John Hulse, the Goostrey parish priest, presided over a service of worship in our private chapel every Sunday at noon, to which the family and their guests, and the estate workers and those servants not engaged in essential duties attended. After this ceremony the traditional Sunday meal of roast meat and vegetables would be served. The Reverend's invariable eagerness to join us for luncheon led my father to speculate that it was his way of ensuring he had at least one decent meal a week.

Well, today wasn't Sunday and although our mystery guest was dressed as a cleric, the good Master Hulse he most certainly was not. I bounded forward and gave my brother a rib-crushing hug.

Giles had been away at theological college for the past year and, as far as I knew, there was another couple to go before he would be let loose on the world as a fully-fledged priest. So what on earth was he doing here? Do neophytes get holidays? Had he failed the course? Oh, what the hell! Whatever the reason, it was good to have the young rascal home again.

It was strange to think how much I had missed him. I never thought anyone could take Ned's place, especially Giles, but the little lad took to following me around so I began to teach him things like how to make a snare and where was the best place to find fish in the river. He showed a genuine interest, which pleased and encouraged me. I loved to see the look of utter pleasure on his face when he successfully trapped a rabbit or landed a big catch. Giles was good company and the older we got the closer we became. Until I left to join the regiment we spent a lot of time together, the willing tutor and the eager pupil.

It was at Ned's funeral that Mother first voiced the idea of Giles being a priest. Perhaps it was her way of coping with grief, but the Giles I knew lived for the here and now, and as far as I know had never given a thought to the hereafter, but she chose to see some sort of divinity in him and, like it or not, he was eventually packed off to theological college. I wondered how the college had changed him, if at all.

'Well, do you think I'll do?' he said, his cheerful voice snapping me out of my reverie.

He clasped his hands together at chest height in a parody of our scholarly vicar. 'Giles Neville, Lay Reader, at your service,' he chanted. 'Duly authorised to assist in the administration of the sacraments and other rites and ceremonies of the church.'

I had to smile, but I felt uneasy.

'Are you happy doing this?' I said.

He shrugged. 'It could be worse. At least in the Church of England a priest doesn't have to be celibate.'

He turned away and began helping himself to the food on the sideboard. I followed his lead and we carried our loaded plates back to the table. Although I was overjoyed to find him here I was more than a bit peeved that no one had told me he was expected.

'I would never have agreed to go off collecting the rents if I'd known you were coming home,' I grumbled when we were seated, looking daggers at my father who, fortunately for me, didn't hear.

'I didn't know myself until the last minute,' he said.

God! It was good to see that raffish grin again.

'I knew I was to be sent to a parish. They do that you know, once you've finished all that boring theory stuff. It's to give you a 'practical experience of ministry',' he said, the last part in a snooty voice. 'I had a sneaking idea of where it was going to be and when it was confirmed I couldn't wait to bring the good news home myself,'

'So tell me, where is this wonderful place?'

His grin grew wider. 'St Luke's. I'm to be

Lay Reader there until I'm ordained as Deacon!'

'St Luke's? Our St Luke's? The one in Goostrey village?'

'The very same. Father arranged it.'

My father cleared his throat. 'It has been obvious to the parochial council for some time that the vicar could do with some help,' he said. 'I simply mentioned it to the bishop that's all.'

'And told him it wouldn't cost the church a penny piece because I'd be non-stipendiary, and I could live at home.'

'That last part was your mother's idea.'

Giles wouldn't let him off the hook. 'The bishop says you offered to pay to restore the bell tower as well.'

My father cleared his throat. 'Any problems with the tenants, Thomas?' he asked, changing the subject.

'I had to draw Seth Seaton's attention to his silage pit. It was leaching into the river.'

My mother entered the room as I was speaking. Elizabeth Neville was a strikingly handsome woman with sharp, cornflower-blue eyes. She was tall and slender and managed to look regal even in the simple homespun clothing she habitually wore about the house.

She wrinkled her nose. 'You will oblige me, Thomas, by not talking about such disgusting things at the breakfast table . . . and you know I don't like Hagar in here when we are eating.'

The dog lay in a pool of warm sunlight beneath the window. Her ears twitched at the mention of her name and she opened one eye, but with no command forthcoming she stretched and with a contented sigh went back to sleep.

'Dear Giles. It is *so* lovely to have you home again,' Mother said, giving my brother a peck on the cheek. 'Fetch me a plate of cold tongue will you? There's a good boy.'

Giles obediently made for the sideboard while my father pulled out a chair so that his wife could join us at the table.

When we were all seated again, she said, 'One would think there would be plenty of carriages for hire in Knutsford, but as Giles will testify, that simply is not so. Isn't that right my darling?'

'I'd still be there now if one of the other passengers hadn't persuaded a passing carter to give us a lift,' Giles said. Then, with a mischievous glance in our mother's direction, he added, winking at me, 'He's a handsome fellow. Mamma was quite taken with him, don't you know. Especially as he took her to be my sister.'

My mother averted her eyes. 'It was as

embarrassing for him as it was for me,' she said, jabbing at the cold meat with her fork. 'But I am indebted to him for seeing my son safely home . . . the least I could do was to invite him to dinner.'

At this remark my father looked up. 'What's that you say? You've invited this fellow to dine with us? Now what do you want to do that for? We don't know him, Eliza. He could be anybody.'

My mother lifted her head in order to look down her nose haughtily at him. 'In actual fact, he is an ordained priest,' she said rather grandly, 'here to visit a poor relation who lives in the village. Now that should tell you something about the sort of person he is . . . Giles dear, you must show him St Luke's. Perhaps he would like to meet the Reverend?'

Giles frowned. 'Er, I don't think that would be a good idea, Mamma,' he said.

'Roman, is he?' my father suggested, sipping his brandy.

'No, definitely Anglican.' Giles countered. 'He's the son of a Church of England rector actually and ordained by the Bishop of Chester himself, but he's, er, got no time for the established church.' He gave a little nervous laugh. 'He says he grew out of it, so he started one of his own.'

51

'The devil he has!' Father said disapprovingly.

My mother chose to ignore him. 'This humble relative of his has no accommodation for guests so he is forced to stay at the tavern. Now, I know Joshua Napper does his best, but his cuisine is hardly suitable for a gentleman.'

My father shot me a searching look. 'Thomas stays at Napper's tavern and he hasn't complained,' he said.

I hunched my shoulders and made a face by pulling down the corners of my mouth. I could see he wasn't happy with the thought of entertaining a complete stranger at his table. He continued to quiz my mother.

'Where is he from, this clerical gentleman?' he asked. 'Do we know his family?'

'Their name is Cruikshank . . . Giles, see if there is some relish will you? There's a dear. This tongue is awfully dry.'

Father was obviously still quite annoyed and struggling to keep his temper. 'Really, Eliza,' he whispered through gritted teeth. 'I can't have you inviting people to dine with us before I have had the chance to make their acquaintance.'

My mother stood up from the table. 'Rupert Neville, you are insufferable!' she said. 'Edwin Cruikshank is coming to dinner and that's final. You can either join us or not, it's up to you. Either way it is of no consequence to me.' And with that she flounced out of the parlour leaving my father speechless.

3

Leaving Giles in the courtyard playing with Hagar, I dragged myself into the great hall where I collapsed into the first chair I came to. We had tramped miles that afternoon, Giles, Hagar and me, across endless fields, through dense woodland and over numerous rivers — or was it over the same river numerous times? I didn't know and I didn't care any more. I dropped my gun and the brace of rabbits we'd bagged on the floor beside me. I was muddy, tired and exhausted — and completely at ease with life. I had just pulled off my boots when Giles came bounding in with Hagar at his side panting happily.

'There's a lot of retriever in this dog, did you see the way she went after those rabbits?'

This was the Giles I knew and loved. His face was aglow and his eyes shining with excitement. I can't remember seeing him so elated since that day in our secret fishing place when it was he who finally caught that cunning old pike.

We had changed into some old clothes for our walk and I marvelled at how far removed this ruddy cheeked, tousled haired youth with torn breeches was from the sombre young man in black of breakfast time. It *was* good to have him home again, and spending the day with him confirmed just what an excellent companion he was — and just how much I had missed him. I reached down for the rabbits.

'Here, you'd better put these on the table before the part of Hagar that's not retriever decides they'd make a tasty meal.'

There was a sudden flurry of activity. Norbury, our butler, appeared followed by two housemaids. One carried a basket and went round replacing every candle in the room with a new one and the other with beeswax and cloth began polishing the long table. Then a gardener came in with his arms full of split logs, which he dumped on the hearth with a loud sigh of relief.

The rabbits were still dangling on my hand. I beckoned the butler over and gave them to him.

'Dining in here tonight are we, Norbury?' I said, which was a fatuous question if there ever was one.

'On her Ladyship's instruction, sir.'

The last person in this world I wanted to sit at table with was the Reverend Cruikshank.

'Mother has got her way again,' I said to Giles.

He shrugged his shoulders. 'Doesn't she always?' There was an uncharacteristic trace of bitterness in his voice. Seeing the look of concern on my face he put on a big grin and said, 'Come on. We had better clean ourselves up otherwise mother's guest will think he has wandered into a den of vagabonds.'

I did consider not going down to dine at all but that would only have led to embarrassing explanations. The only thing to do was to brazen it out, and let's face it, my mother's guest was hardly likely to bring up the subject of seducing Josh Napper's daughter at the dinner table. I resolved not make conversation but to be polite if spoken to.

As it turned out, Edwin Cruikshank acted as if we had never met before. He strode into the great hall with all the confidence in the world, completely ignoring Giles and me, making straight for my parents and greeting them both like old friends.

My father looked puzzled, as if he had met him somewhere before but couldn't recall the time and place. Eventually, with a shake of his head, he gave up and completed the introductions. Cruikshank made a great fuss of seeing Giles again but said nothing more than a polite, 'How do you do,' to me, which suited me very well.

Finch came in carrying a basket. 'Ah! Finch!' Cruikshank exclaimed. 'Well, don't just stand there. Set it down man, set it down.'

The former sergeant looked at me and rolled his eyes. Clearly he shared my opinion of this bumptious fellow. I slipped him a wink.

Resting on top of the basket was a posy of wild flowers. Cruikshank handed this to my mother with a flourish.

'For you, madam,' he said. 'Pretty flowers for a pretty lady.'

She blushed and looked a little uncomfortable. He then reached into the basket and drew out a dark green bottle sealed with wax.

'And this is my sister's elderflower cordial. I guarantee you will like it.'

I never doubted that he would make an entertaining dinner guest and, although prejudiced, I had to admit his conversation at table was amusing and witty. He spoke softly but his voice had strength and a lilt that was almost hypnotic, and there was not a subject upon which he could not converse. Giles was clearly impressed by him, and he seemed to have completely captivated my mother. He would occasionally lean over, top up her glass from the green bottle and whisper something that made her blush like a schoolgirl, which I found embarrassing. I wondered how long it would be before my father noticed. Good looks and a smooth tongue would cut no ice with the down-to-earth ex-magistrate. I could hardly wait for him to put this self-assured seducer in his place.

We had reached the dessert stage and baked apple pudding, a family favourite, was just being served when, right out of the blue, Cruikshank said, 'You are to be congratulated, Sir Rupert.'

At that precise moment my father was more interested in whether Giles would leave enough pudding for him to have a second helping. 'Oh, really?' he said rather absently.

Our guest went on, 'From what I have seen of the countryside hereabouts I would say your estate is remarkably well managed.'

That was right on target. The baked apple pudding suddenly became of secondary importance and Father turned to our guest, his face beaming.

'It's all down to having the right people as your tenants,' he said modestly, 'and I can't take the credit for that. Some of them have been here longer than me.'

My mother took the arrival of a decanter of port as the signal for her to retire, her husband giving her an almost imperceptible nod of approval as she stood up.

'They are all doing well, with one exception. Isn't that right, Thomas?'

'They are indeed, sir,' I replied. 'Our only problem is the Craddock farm.'

His face clouded. 'And that's a problem that has to be resolved, my boy. Nathan Craddock's wife dying last winter seems to have knocked all the stuffing out of the poor fellow.' He turned to Cruikshank. 'She was all he had you see, they had never been blessed with children.'

'I heard his cowman is keen to take over the tenancy,' I offered.

'Who, Big Ernie?' Giles asked, sceptically.

My father nodded his head solemnly. 'Yes, that's right. I know Ernest Goodrich is not very bright but he's strong, hardworking and honest, and he's worked on that farm for thirty years. I can't think of anyone better qualified to take the place over — but his daughters won't want to share the farmhouse with old Nathan.'

'Whoever takes the tenancy on won't want a crabby old man under their feet and that's for sure,' Giles said, reaching for the decanter.

My father shot him a reproachful look. 'It's not Craddock's fault he's old and the last of his line, damn it!'

'What about your plans to build alms-houses?' I suggested. 'Isn't that on your list of 'good works'?'

Cruikshank was quick to pick this up. 'What a capital idea, Sir Rupert!' he gushed. 'Surely it's just a matter of finding temporary accommodation for this Nathan Craddock until the project is completed?'

My father rose from the table and crossed over to the fireplace. He selected a long-stemmed, 'churchwarden', clay pipe from a rack on the mantelpiece and began to fill its small bowl with tobacco.

'I'm afraid that's only a dream, Master Cruikshank,' he said sadly. 'Every year the money I put aside in the building fund gets used up on something more pressing, repairs to a cottage, or a new roof for a barn . . .'

Giles gave me a nudge. 'Or the church bell tower needs refurbishing,' he whispered.

Cruikshank joined my father at the fireplace. He stooped to light a taper in the glowing embers. Hagar, who was stretched out in front of the fire, raised her head and growled menacingly.

'Then I venture to suggest that you increase your income, Sir Rupert,' the cleric said, straightening up with the flame.

The pipe was lit and a long plume of white smoke drifted up the wide chimney.

'I won't put up rents,' my father said, vehemently.

'Then make your money work for you.'

'I'll have nothing to do with the stock market, not after so many good people were ruined by the South Sea Bubble.'

Giles sat up. 'The South Sea Bubble! What on earth is that?'

'Was,' Cruikshank said languidly. 'It all happened nearly twenty years ago. The South Sea Company was formed on a wildly optimistic view of trading prospects with South America. It undertook to pay off the national debt in return for a guarantee of a trading monopoly in those parts. When the word got out, everyone wanted a part of this fabulous crock of gold and in the first few months the Company's share value rocketed, but because the whole scheme was based on expectation and not on reality, within the year the bubble had burst . . . '

'And countless small investors were made bankrupt,' my father added grimly. 'Some poor souls killed themselves.'

Edwin Cruikshank smiled. 'Everyone knows the value of shares can go down as well as up, sir, the trick is knowing when to buy and when to sell. I bought South Sea Company shares in the January, by July their price had increased tenfold — that was when I sold.'

Giles whistled. There was an undisguised look of admiration on his young face. 'And you made a lot of money?'

'I made a fortune,' our guest replied, casually.

We talked until our supply of logs ran out. It was only when we began to feel the cold did we think of joining my mother in the comfort of her withdrawing room. Norbury was just leaving her as we walked in.

'Do you realise what hour it is?' she said to my father, her eyes flashing angrily. 'The Nappers will have gone to bed long since and their house will be locked and barred for the night. Master Cruikshank has no alternative but to stay here. I've instructed Norbury to have the small room above the porch made up for him.'

Our guest went through the motions of protesting politely, saying he didn't want to put anyone to any trouble.

'You will be comfortable in the porch room, Master Cruikshank,' she said firmly. 'Rupert prefers to sleep in the east wing, he claims it's warmer there, but my chamber is on that side of the house, just the other side of the prayer room.'

She looked at him from under her lashes and smiled coquettishly. I turned away. I couldn't bear to watch my mother behaving like a silly moonstruck girl.

★ ★ ★

I avoid breakfast whenever I can when I'm home on leave. Far better to grab a lump of game pie and a flask of ale from the kitchen and escape into the fields with a gun on my shoulder and Hagar at my heels than to get the silent treatment from one parent and disapproving looks from the other. But with a guest in the house it would have been ill mannered not to put in an appearance.

I was however, in no hurry to be in the company of the Reverend Cruikshank so I dallied a bit over my toilet and in consequence I was the last down to the sun-lit parlour where, surprisingly, not only was there talk, but laughter as well.

Giles was the one doing all the talking and it was my mother who was laughing. For some reason Hagar refused to cross the threshold which caused me to hesitate in the doorway, and from there I was possibly the only one to see the expression on Mother's face change to one of intimate tenderness as she looked across to the sideboard where Cruikshank was filling his plate.

He seemed more cocksure than ever, if that were possible.

'May I compliment you, sir, on the fine collection of portraits you have in the gallery upstairs,' he said to my father as he took a seat at the table. 'I would dearly like to know more about them.'

He'd done it again. I watched Father grow taller in his chair. Sir Rupert was immensely proud of his family's ancient name and had over a dozen paintings of its most important members hanging in the long gallery. As boys, Giles and me would refer to them as the 'dead Nevilles', but never in our father's hearing.

He smiled at our guest. 'My dear sir, I will be delighted . . . I say, give that bell pull a tug, there's a good fellow. Norbury seems to have forgotten my brandy.'

Cruikshank reached into the pocket of his coat and produced a flask of finely chased silver. 'Pray, accept mine, Sir Rupert. It is the finest cognac, I never travel without it.'

He poured a generous measure into a glass. My father sipped the spirit and nodded his head appreciatively.

'We can look at the portraits after breakfast if you like. It won't take long, then Finch can drive you back to Goostrey.' He drained the contents of the glass. 'I'll tell you what, I'll have my sons give you the guided tour, let's see what they remember about the family tree . . . I say, I appear to have finished this brandy.'

★ ★ ★

The first baronet, Sir John Neville, added the south wing of the house during the reign of Good Queen Bess and, as was the fashion in those days, a long gallery was included as a place for daily exercise and games. Originally, this impressive seventy-foot long room at the top of the newel staircase would have been sparsely furnished but now, in addition to the rows of paintings in heavy, gilded frames, there were sofas and chairs spaced at intervals along its walls. Giles winked at me when we were all assembled.

'Shall I go first?' he asked innocently. I smiled back at him knowing that my brother's knowledge of our family's history was at least equal to that of our father's.

'You can begin, Giles,' my father replied. 'But I want Thomas to do his share.'

I groaned inwardly, but I shouldn't have worried, for when Giles got underway there was no stopping him. For once even Cruikshank was content to listen as my little brother trotted out the facts in a light-hearted and entertaining way that only he could get away with. He paused in front of a large equine portrait.

'Alderman Geoffrey de Neville, three times Mayor of Congleton,' he intoned in an affected, 'boorish lecturer' voice and then, dropping back into his own jocular way of speaking, added, 'He looks quite impressive sitting on that horse doesn't he? You wouldn't think he was only five feet two.'

I managed to smother a laugh but my father glowered at him. 'He may have been small but the estate doubled in size under his stewardship,' he said angrily.

'Yes, by buying up land as it came on the market after the Black Death.'

Cruikshank smiled. 'How very enterprising of him,' he said.

Giles strode off down the gallery and beckoned Cruikshank to follow him. My father and I tagged along behind.

'You admire enterprise Master Cruikshank?' Giles said, with a mischievous gleam in his eye. 'Then allow me to present Hartley Neville or 'Hartley the Heartless' as he was known hereabouts.'

With an exaggerated wave of his hand he indicated a small picture in a most elaborate frame from which a bewhiskered and rather stern-looking man in sombre Tudor dress

66

glowered out at us.

'Hartley was Henry VIII's tax collector in these parts. Having friends at Court meant that when the King dissolved the monasteries he was well placed to get hold of the land adjoining the estate that was Church owned. By the end of the Reformation the amount of Neville property had doubled yet again.'

Cruikshank linked arms with my father and led him off some thirty feet to the end of the gallery where there was a large window. This was obviously intended to be a private moment so Giles and I remained where we were, both knowing that the acoustics in the long gallery were such that we would still hear every word they said anyway.

'Land taken from the dead and land taken from the Church. Do you know, Sir Rupert, I'm beginning to like your family.'

Cruikshank positioned my father in front of the window, which he took the liberty of opening. We were three floors up and there was an excellent view across the Cheshire plain to the hills of Derbyshire in the distance.

'Tell me, how far does your land extend in this direction?' he asked.

'Not very far actually, just a few miles beyond the old priory. You can just make out the ruins beyond that stand of trees.'

'What if I said you could own everything as far as the eye can see?'

'I'd say you were talking rubbish, sir! Even if the owners were prepared to sell, I couldn't possibly afford to buy so much land.'

Cruikshank ignored his protest. 'Just imagine, Sir Rupert, *your* portrait up there along with Alderman Geoffrey, King Henry's tax collector and Sir John the first baronet . . . And here, ladies and gentlemen, we have Sir Rupert, the greatest Neville of them all,' he said, giving a very good impersonation of Giles who was biting his fist to stifle a guffaw. 'Don't worry about the present owners not being willing to sell. Everyone has a price. All you need is money.'

'And just how am I supposed to get this money?'

There was a degree of exasperation in my father's voice but the thoughtful look on his face told me that Cruikshank had him interested.

'A wise man will always heed the advice of an expert. You need money and you need it quickly. Put your trust in me, Sir Rupert. Let me be your expert and I will show you how easy it is to get what you want in this life.' He paused to study my father and he seemed pleased with what he saw. 'First we will have those almshouses and after that, who knows . . . '

'I wish he'd show me how to get what I want,' Giles whispered.

I signalled to him to be quiet as my father was speaking. He was asking Cruikshank what he would advise him to do. Our guest had baited his line with some tasty titbits. Not only had he offered my father the means to build the almshouses he dearly wanted and more land than he had ever dreamed of but he was also tempting him with something no man could refuse, immortality. It may have sounded like a joke but I saw the look on my father's face when he hinted that future generations would see him as the greatest Neville of them all. By God, he wanted that — and Cruikshank knew it! The smooth bastard had him hooked as surely as Giles's pike was that day in our secret fishing place.

'We have no time to lose,' he said. 'I take it you have plans drawn up for these alms-houses?'

'Yes, and the site mapped out but I don't have money for the materials.'

'Use the building fund money! Go now and buy the bricks and whatever else you need to get the job started. Don't look so shocked, Sir Rupert, the Bishop will still get his new bell tower.'

'How can I possibly fund both projects?'

Cruikshank put his arm around my father's

shoulder and lowered his voice slightly. 'There is to be a prizefight at Holmes Chapel on Saturday,' he said.

My father shook himself free. 'I can't be seen gambling! I'm a member of the parochial council.'

'Then send a proxy, a lot of people do.' The cleric held out his hands in a gesture of supplication. 'Look, I know the contestants. I've had many a wager on both of them. Put your money on Jem Mace. This is no gamble, trust me.'

Norbury appeared at the top of the stairs.

'Her ladyship has asked me to inform you, sir, that Finch has the carriage ready.'

'It would seem that I have to leave you.' Cruikshank said with a resigned smile. 'Think about what I have said. I'll be at the milling field in Holmes Chapel, Saturday evening at nine.'

He walked back up the gallery leaving my father standing by the window deep in thought, when he drew level with Giles he stopped and looked at him appraisingly.

'I have a feeling you will get everything you want in life young man, possibly more than you bargained for,' he said.

4

As the week progressed, my father grew more edgy and tense. When Saturday finally arrived, I was summoned to his study and found him standing in front of the fireplace looking up at the elaborate overmantle.

'I've always liked this room,' he said. 'There's not a finer chimneypiece in the whole house.'

The fireplace in my father's study is smaller than in other rooms but none is more finely moulded. In Sir John's day it was prudent to show one's allegiance to the Crown by displaying the Queen's coat of arms over the hearth in the principle reception room but for his inner sanctum, my ancestor evidently preferred his own heraldic insignia.

'*Fortis fortuna adiuvat,*' my father said, reading aloud the inscription under the shield.

I'd had the family motto drummed into me from being a child. 'Fortune favours the brave,' I said.

He turned and smiled at me. 'That's right, Thomas. Fortune favours the brave or, he who dares, wins.' Thrusting a satchel at me he said, 'Edwin Cruikshank will be at the milling field at nine, take this to him, he knows what to do with it.'

His eyes had a wild look in them, which I found unnerving.

'Are you seriously going ahead with the wager?' I blurted out, quite forgetting that I wasn't supposed to have been eavesdropping.

He didn't seem to notice. 'Yes I am,' he said, 'Cruikshank is so sure his man will win he said to put all the rent money on him.'

I was about to point out that we knew nothing about this smooth talking stranger when he went on.

'So I shall be brave . . . but not foolhardy. I'll risk half.'

His mind was obviously made up and I was about to leave when he said, 'Take Giles with you.'

Yes, Giles would enjoy watching a prize-fight. I wished I'd thought of it.

'Good idea, Father,' I said.

He was back staring at the chimneypiece. 'It was Cruikshank's idea,' he said.

★ ★ ★

Although I was no stranger to the field in Holmes Chapel where the roads from Chester and London meet, at that time of night I'd feel a lot happier to have Sergeant Finch with me. Even half the rent was still a lot of money.

On the way to the stables I met Giles and asked him if he'd like to come.

His eyes shone with excitement. 'Would I ever?' he cried. 'I've always wanted to go to a prizefight.'

'Then for goodness sake change into something that's not clerical black,' I said. 'It isn't a prayer meeting we're going to.'

Seeing the milling field again would be like old times. Before I went away to school, Finch would take me there to watch the fights — without my mother's knowledge of course, for she would have never approved of him teaching me fisticuffs.

'Being a gentleman isn't going to protect you from bullies, Master Thomas,' he told me.

I would meet him secretly in the stables for instruction in the noble art and occasionally we would slip away to study the professionals in action. The milling field was a man's place and to go there made me feel very grown up.

It was strangely pleasing to see that it hadn't changed much over the years. There was a good assembly of elegant coaches on the field, the occupants still divided by class. The coachmen and other flunkeys were huddled together in little groups by the horses, smoking and talking whilst their passengers paced the turf, drinking and laughing and exchanging good-natured banter with others of similar social standing.

Leaving Finch to tie up our horses I set off with Giles to find Edwin Cruikshank, which, as it turned out, was incredibly easy. We simply walked up to the largest and noisiest group and there he was, the centre of attraction as usual. He was dressed in a brown moleskin coat of exquisite cut, a gold-coloured, silk waistcoat, a ruffed, white shirt, white breeches and stockings and brown high-heeled shoes with silver buckles.

Catching sight of us he shouted, 'Forgive me, everyone. I must leave you now. I've just seen the people I've been waiting for.' He came over. 'Did your father send the money?' he asked.

There was a note of urgency in his voice and when I showed him the satchel he almost snatched it from me. He squeezed the bag lovingly and with his eyes closed, whispered a triumphant, 'Yes!' Then, with a shouted, 'I'll see you both at the ringside,' he disappeared into the crowd.

People were beginning to make their way to the middle of the field. I called to Finch to come with us and we went along with the flow, eventually becoming part of a ring of spectators, the space inside lit by a half dozen servants holding flaming torches. Cruikshank suddenly appeared on the far side and ignoring the good-natured jeers and whistles, hurried across the clearing to join us, elbowing his way into the crush to stand at my side.

'Right!' he announced, a little breathlessly. 'Your father's money is on Jem Mace.'

He seemed a bit put out. 'I expected your father's stake to be higher. I did tell him there was nothing to worry about.'

From the scraps of the conversations going on around me I gathered the favourite to win tonight's fight was a pugilist from the next county who was referred to as the Staffordshire Bull. Jem Mace had travelled up from London and was not known here, except to Edwin Cruikshank of course.

The promoter, master of ceremonies and referee for the occasion was the young Marquess of Bexton. Cheers greeted him as he entered the ring.

'My lords and gentlemen,' he shouted. 'Tonight we have a match between Jack Broadbottom, better known to you as the Staffordshire Bull . . . ' A mighty roar went up from the crowd. 'And from London, the Brixton Battler, Jem Mace!'

A ripple of polite clapping plus a few catcalls followed this last announcement. His lordship then proceeded to scratch a line across the middle of the ring with his cane.

'What's he doing that for?' Giles asked, straining to get a better view.

'The fighters begin the bout toeing that line, face to face,' I explained. 'At a signal from the referee they begin slogging away at each other until one of them goes down.'

'Is that it then?' He looked disappointed.

'Good heavens, no. They resume the starting position and the fight goes on. Eventually, when one of them can't come up to the scratch the other is declared the winner.'

The combatants entered the ring to loud applause. The Staffordshire Bull was a fleshy giant of a man who made the sinewy Jem Mace look quite lightweight. I fervently hoped Edwin Cruikshank knew what he was doing. When the contest began and Mace began to dance around his lumbering opponent, landing blow after stinging blow I began to see that he most certainly did.

The fight only lasted an hour, which was disappointing for the spectators. What was even more disappointing for them was that Jem Mace won.

Cruikshank looked upon the losers with

contempt. 'I'll go and collect our winnings then,' he said, stepping into the ring.

Giles fell into step beside him leaving Finch and me to follow. 'Have *you* won much?' he asked.

'But of course, I always do.'

Broadbottom's seconds were trying desperately to get the big man back on his feet. Mace stood watching them dispassionately, his half-naked body, wet and shiny in the flickering torchlight. Cruikshank tapped him on the arm with his cane and whispered something that caused him to laugh, at the same time placing a small purse into the fighter's hand. Mace nodded to him, touching a knuckle to his forehead.

We were making for a group of men standing in a huddle by one of the more impressive carriages. It obviously belonged to an important family but I didn't recognise the coachman's livery or the coat of arms painted on the door. It was apparent that wagers were being honoured and a great amount of money was changing hands with purses being deposited in a heap just inside the open door of the carriage. Two of the men walked away looking very downcast whereas a third appeared very pleased with himself. He was an elegantly dressed fop with a powdered wig who would have looked more at home gracing some fashionable salon instead of soiling his satin shoes in a muddy field. Cruikshank introduced him as Sir Vivian Rushford.

'This is Captain Thomas Neville,' he said to the dandy. 'Son and heir to Sir Rupert Neville of Cheshire.'

It would not have surprised me if Edwin Cruikshank's friend had produced a quizzing glass, as it was he took his time eyeing me up and down appraisingly. His slightly puffy face had a distinctly unhealthy, dissipated look about it. When he spoke it was in a high voice with an affected drawl, which did nothing to improve my opinion of him.

'I've heard of the Nevilles of Cheshire, of course, but I've never met your father. I may call on him whilst I am in the county.' He said this as if he were about to bestow some great honour on the family.

Cruikshank continued. 'And this is his brother, Giles.'

A ghost of a smile flitted across Rushford's plump sensuous lips and I was instantly forgotten as he switched all of his attention to my brother.

'You must be the one taking Holy Orders?' he said, looking at Giles as if he were judging a horse.

Rushford took him to one side and out of

earshot. He whispered something to him to which Giles smiled and nodded his head. My little brother seemed to be flattered by this popinjay's attention but it sent a cold shiver down my spine.

Reaching inside the carriage, Cruikshank produced my father's satchel, which he proceeded to fill with purses of coin from the heap. It became so full that by the time he was finished he had difficulty in fastening it.

Passing it to me, he said, 'Take this to your father. Perhaps in future he will be more trusting.' Then, as an afterthought, he reached into the coach again, this time bringing out a bottle and with a charming smile, he added, 'To show there are no hard feelings, give him this with my compliments . . . I know he has a taste for good brandy.'

* * *

If I had laid a wager as to what my father's reaction would be when we got home I would have lost my money, but then, on the very rare occasions that I gamble, I invariably do. Without a word to either Giles or myself, he snatched the bag and brushing aside the papers that lay on the top of his desk he spilled out its contents onto its shiny, wooden surface. The coins glinted and gleamed in the candlelight. A few rolled onto the floor but he ignored them and began counting and stacking them in neat little piles. When he finished he opened Cruikshank's bottle of brandy and poured himself a large measure, which he tossed down his throat.

'Damn me for not having the nerve to bet all the money,' he said.

I stared at him in disbelief. Was this really my father, the former magistrate and a member of the church council who is renowned for his prudence and good sense?

'But we knew nothing about Edwin Cruikshank, you said so yourself.'

'Well, he clearly knew what he was talking about and I should never have doubted him,' he mumbled and began rummaging among the untidy pile of papers on his desk. 'We'll begin work on those almshouses first thing tomorrow, Thomas. You don't have to go back to your regiment just yet, do you?'

'I've still got two days leave, sir.'

'There's everything you'll need here, architect's drawings, site plans, surveyors reports.'

For a moment I thought I saw that wild look in his eyes again but he gave me no time to ponder on it. 'Go and see that architect fellow, Ashley,' he said. 'And tell him I want him to put the work in hand immediately — immediately, understand? And make sure he knows it's almshouses I want, almshouses pure and simple. The damned fellow keeps trying to talk me into building a workhouse!'

Giles had been standing open-mouthed. 'But this is *your* 'good work', sir,' he exclaimed. 'Surely you'll want to see to the arrangements yourself.'

'*I*, sir, will be visiting Master Cruikshank! It's only polite to tender one's thanks for a favour, is it not?'

My little brother clearly didn't take this as a rebuke. He smiled innocently and said, 'You can save yourself the trouble, Father. He's coming here. A friend of his at the prizefight asked me to present his compliments to you and to say he will be calling on you tomorrow. I was given to understand that Edwin Cruikshank would be with him . . . something about asking Mamma to show him the ruined priory.'

Father stopped sorting through his papers. 'Who is this friend of Master Cruikshank?' he asked.

'A fellow called Rushford . . . Comes from a good family.'

'Rushford? I don't know the name but if he's a friend of Cruikshank, he is welcome at Dunmere Hall.'

When I gave Jacob Ashley my father's instruction to go ahead with the almshouses he was so overcome he didn't quite know what to do. For a minute or two he paced his small, cold room punching his fist into his hand and muttering to himself. Then he regained his composure and after clearing his throat he opened a thick ledger on his desk and made a show of reading the entries on its pages.

'My compliments to Sir Rupert and kindly tell him that I am available to accept this commission,' he said at length.

Pompous ass, I thought. The frayed jacket cuffs and darns in his hose spoke of hard times. I didn't know if he had any other work on but he did have a large family and I was pleased to think that this project would at least see them with food and warmth through the winter.

Ashley stroked his moustache thoughtfully. 'It is after all, your father's business what he chooses to spend his money on,' he continued. 'But you might remind him of my alternative suggestion. It would involve some alteration to the plans but I'm sure the elderly would benefit by having some simple tasks to perform in return for their keep . . . Indeed if we put the right master in charge.' He paused to give me a conspiratorial smile and a wink. 'Your father may even see a profit.'

I was pleased my father had warned me of this possibility. I didn't like the way this man's mind worked and I made no attempt to hide my feelings.

'It is Sir Rupert's wish to give shelter and comfort to people who have spent their lives working for the estate,' I said. 'Not to exploit their vulnerability. My father wants you to build almshouses, Master Ashley. Almshouses, pure and simple. Good day to you, sir.'

★ ★ ★

I had rather expected to see Rushford's opulent carriage when I got back to the hall but the stable yard was empty. I asked Sergeant Finch if the visit had in fact taken place after all.

'Indeed it did, sir,' he said. 'In fact they're still here . . . well not *here* exactly, if you know what I mean. Lady Neville has gone off in the gig with Master Cruikshank — I did offer to drive, sir, but she said I wasn't needed — and Sir Rupert and Master Giles have gone to a race meeting on Knutsford Heath with the other gentleman, in his carriage.'

Leaving my horse with Finch, I went full of thought into the house. I accept that being heir to the Neville estate has its responsibilities and when I am home I expect to do my share, like collecting the rent the other day, for instance. But it did seem unfair that I should be working while everyone else was off enjoying themselves. A day at the races would have made a very agreeable end to my leave.

I changed into some old clothes and took my gun into the fields. This pleased Hagar who ran back and forth in front of me making little happy, yelping noises. I didn't set off in any particular direction; I just walked. I crossed lush pastures dotted with cows where the grass was short and through meadows where it was knee-high and full of wild flowers.

We were crossing a large field when a woodpigeon suddenly lifted off immediately in front of us with a great flapping of wings. Hagar was quick to recover from the shock and was after it like a shot. The big bird worked hard to gain height and was soon able to glide safely into the distance. By way of consolation I picked up a stick and threw it for the dog. The woodpigeon was instantly forgotten as she ran off to retrieve it. This was one of her favourite games and I knew I would tire of it long before she did.

I don't know how long I walked but as I

stepped out of a small copse I heard the sound of laughter, woman's laughter. The old priory lay ahead of me. I snapped my fingers and signalled Hagar to heel. Finch said that my mother had gone to the priory with Edwin Cruikshank. There was another sound, a flute or a pipe of some sort. Quietly whispering to Hagar to lie down, I moved forward, and then I saw them.

He was in his shirtsleeves playing a panpipe and she was dancing barefoot, with flowers in her hair like some silly shepherdess in one of Antoine Watteau's romantic *fête galante* paintings. I could hardly believe my own eyes. My mother was actually dancing for that arrogant seducer! An angry red mist clouded the vision and I found myself furiously ramming powder and shot down the barrel of the gun. Trembling with rage I levelled the primed weapon at Cruikshank, but at that moment a great black rook flew in through the ruined walls of the priory and I vented my anger by blasting the poor bird out of the sky. It fell at my mother's feet, a twitching heap of blood and feathers. She screamed and Cruikshank swept her up in his arms to comfort her. His soulless eyes searched the line of trees for the marksman, but I had long since stepped back into the anonymity of their shadows.

To this day I don't know if I would have shot him. I gave Hagar a low whistle and we set off back to the hall at the slow, loping run that a sergeant in the Cheshires had introduced me to. He claimed the natives of the American colonies could maintain it for hours and still fight a battle at the end of it. I tried it and I believed him. The stride was longer and slower than the British Army's regulation 'double time', enabling a body of men to cover ground quickly but also silently and without getting seriously out of breath. The whole of my company, including the officers, were well practiced in it although we still marched 'at the double' for drill purposes.

As I approached the stables I could see Rushford's coach in the yard with Sergeant Finch and the knight's liveried driver walking the steaming horses in the paddock.

''Tis no way to treat such magnificent beasts,' Finch grumbled when I got to him. He nodded his head in the direction of the coachman.

'This fellow says his master insisted on driving the coach back from the races himself and he went so fast you'd a'thought Old Nick was chasing him.'

Leaving Hagar in Finch's safe keeping, I went up to the house. Giles must have seen me coming as he came running out to meet me. He was grinning from ear to ear.

'You missed some good sport at Knutsford,' he shouted while there was still some distance between us. 'Vivian marked Father's card and the old man won a bundle!'

'Where is everyone?' I asked.

He fell into step beside me. 'We had to put Father to bed. He's had one too many . . . Vivian's in the great hall.'

My brother was slurring his words, which led me to think that perhaps Father was not the only one who had over indulged.

'And Mamma?'

'She didn't come with us.'

'I know, I just wondered if she was back that's all.'

He sniggered into his hand. 'She'll not be home yet awhile. She's at the old priory with Edwin Cruikshank.' He winked and nudged me with his elbow. 'Those ruins can be very romantic at sundown.'

We had reached the door to the hall porch. The vision of her dancing barefoot with flowers in her hair was still very fresh in my memory. I grabbed his arm and pulled him round to face me.

'Steady on, Giles!' I said. 'This *is* our mother you're talking about . . . and you a man of the cloth!'

He pouted his lips. 'Everyone is entitled to a little bit of fun, old chap. It'll do Mamma's ego the power of good to have an attractive man paying court to her . . . And don't worry about Father, I've never seen the old boy enjoy himself as much as he did today.' He wriggled out of my grip and opened the door. 'Fortune smiled on the Nevilles the day Edwin Cruikshank came into our lives,' he called back over his shoulder. 'He's brought some much needed gaiety into this dull old place.'

When I thought about it I had to admit Giles was right. Never have I seen my parents enjoying life quite as much as they were at the moment. My mother behaving like a silly schoolgirl embarrassed me, but was I being overly prudish and perhaps even a little selfish? God knows she deserves some happiness and if a flirtation with a good-looking man makes her happy who am I to deny her the pleasure. And as for my father, well, he wasn't bothered and if it weren't for Cruikshank he wouldn't be acquiring the means to put his 'good works' into practice — and by the sound of it, enjoying the experience.

I can well understand young Giles being in awe of the strikingly handsome priest. Here was a man who was slightly larger than life, full of confidence and *joie de vivre*; one of those people for whom everything in life seems to go right and when you were in his company you somehow felt that things were going right for you as well. If I didn't hate him for seducing Emily I'd probably be under his spell too.

In the great hall, I could see Rushford sprawled in a chair by the fireplace, smoking a long churchwarden. With a great whoop, Giles ran in to him but I wasn't in the mood for skylarking so I went up the servant's staircase to my room.

It was the last night of my leave and as it looked very much as though Cruikshank and his friend would be joining us for dinner I decided to swank a bit and wear my regimentals. I had just pulled on my boots when I heard the rumble of wheels on the bridge. I went to the window and looked out. Finch was there of course and I watched as he stepped forward to hold the horse's head while Edwin Cruikshank got down to assist my mother as she alighted from the gig. She was talking non-stop, her free hand fluttering in the air one moment and clamping itself to her heaving bosom the next. I could hardly believe that this vivacious, demonstrative woman I was looking at was that same staid and reserved mother who had never given me so much as a hug.

I was right about Cruikshank and his friend dining with us and it didn't surprise me when Norbury informed me that they had also been invited to stay the night. I was not, however, expecting the bombshell that my father was to drop on us later.

Mother seemed to have recovered from her shock at the priory, which relieved me no end. She recounted the event over dinner.

'And suddenly, there was a gunshot,' she said, pausing for effect and looking around the table for a reaction to this dramatic announcement. 'Are we being set upon by bandits or robbers? I cried. 'Fear not', said my companion, 'for I will protect you.''

She gave Cruikshank a winning smile. His hand was resting on the table and she leaned forward and gave it a squeeze. The incident wasn't quite as I remembered it but not being in any position to argue I had to let it go.

'Dear, courageous Edwin was ready to fight off a whole company of brigands if need be,' she continued. 'But there was no more gunfire and the only casualty was a poor little bird.'

Hardly a little bird, I thought. The ugly brute must have weighed at least a pound and a half.

'A sneak-thief poacher, nothing more,' said

her hero modestly. He looked straight at me, his soulless eyes telling me he knew I was the marksman.

My father rose rather unsteadily to his feet and raised his glass. He stood for a long embarrassing moment with a silly grin on his face.

'A toast to my son who is off to rejoin his regiment,' he said. He smiled at me and I was surprised to see a look of genuine affection on his flushed face. His next remark was to surprise me even more. 'And a toast to my good friends, Edwin Cruikshank and Vivian Rushford, who, for as long as they are in the county are most welcome to use Dunmere Hall as their home.'

5

It was Christmas Eve. I left the barracks at dawn but it was slow going. There had been a fall of snow overnight and by the time I reached Holmes Chapel the sun was high in the sky.

At the junction of the two major roads I stopped and stood in the saddle to have a look around. A glistening coat of white covered everything, beautiful on the fields, but treacherous in the sun dappled lanes where it concealed wagon ruts and potholes. My horse had stumbled a few times but the faithful animal had brought me this far without mishap. I gave him a few words of encouragement, patted his neck and moved him on. The road here was particularly nasty with a layer of snow concealing ice beneath. The inevitable happened and my gallant horse went down. I quickly slid from the saddle and he was up and walking again in no time, but with a worrying limp. Napper's tavern was but a few miles away so I decided to walk my horse there and pick up a fresh mount from Josh's stable.

As we entered Goostrey village my

thoughts were of Emily, as they so often were. She was always my first thought in the morning and my last before going to sleep. I couldn't leave things as they were. I had to talk to her. She wasn't the first young girl to be led astray, and she certainly wouldn't be the last. A simple country girl in the first flush of womanhood was easy prey for a practiced charmer like Cruikshank.

Someone had been busy clearing the snow from the yard, the sort of thing Emily would do without bidding. I felt my heart quicken at the prospect of coming face to face with her in the next few seconds. I had so convinced myself that it would be Emily's sweet face I would see when the stable door opened that I was disappointed when it turned out to be old Simon who answered my call.

For my horse's sake though I was glad he was here. A grumpy old man he may be but even Sergeant Finch would agree that there wasn't a better horse doctor in the whole of Cheshire. I told him about the fall at the crossroads and at his insistence I walked the horse back and forth across the yard. Signalling me to stop he came forward and gently lifted the injured foreleg.

He whispered to the horse, running his fingers expertly over muscles and tendons. After a while he said, 'There's nothing here that a bit of rest won't put right.'

I was greatly relieved to hear that. 'I'll have to borrow one of your hacks to finish my journey,' I said. 'Sort me out a decent one and put my saddle on it, there's a good fellow. I'll square it with Josh.'

'Folk should have more sense than to travel the roads in this weather,' he grumbled.

Choosing to ignore the remark, I asked casually, 'Is Emily around?'

'You haven't heard then.'

Something must have happened to her. Old Simon could be infuriating at times and I regret to say I found myself shouting at him.

'Good God, man! I've been away for almost three months. What haven't I heard?'

'She's gone away.'

'Gone away! Gone where, for pity's sake.'

He screwed his leathery old face into a grim smile and lowered his voice. 'Ah, there you has it, sir,' he said. 'Nobody knows.'

This was devastating news. I had to find Josh. If anyone knew Emily's whereabouts it would be him. I had one last question for Simon before I went into the tavern.

'When did this happen?' I asked.

'Yesterday it were. She had a blazing row with one of the customers and that was the last anyone saw of her.'

* * *

The taproom was as silent as a tomb and just about as convivial. I opened the door expecting the usual buzz of conversation but there was nothing. The only thing of any cheer was the fire in the hearth. Two ancient yokels sat in the inglenook smoking their pipes and silently contemplating their corpulent host who was slumped dejectedly at a table by the window. Other than those three, the place was deserted.

Josh looked up as I came in. 'If you've come for the rent, Master Thomas, your father's bailiff has already been,' he said belligerently.

'What's this about Emily, Josh?'

His head slumped forward and his big shoulders shook. I could never have envisaged big, jovial Josh Napper with tears running down his ruddy cheeks. To witness it was one of the saddest experiences of my life. There was a jug of ale on the table and some tankards. I filled one of them and placed it beside him. He sniffed loudly and wiped his face with a podgy hand.

'She's walked out on me,' he said.

'Did she say where she was going?'

'No, she just went.'

'I heard she had a row with someone.'

'Only one of my best customers!' he said

angrily, snatching up the tankard. He downed most of its contents and set it back on the table with a thump. A dribble of ale ran down his chin, which he ignored.

'I know Master Cruikshank lives at the hall now but him and his friends still use this place a lot. And she knows how much money they spends in here. The silly girl should have kept a still tongue in her head.'

'What did they argue about?' I asked.

The big man's anger left him as quickly as it had come and there was desperation in his voice when he replied. 'I don't know! Emily wasn't there to ask and Master Cruikshank, being the gentleman he is, just laughed it off, said it was nothing.'

He looked up at me with fear in his red-rimmed eyes. 'I must find her,' he said. 'I can't just do nothing while she's out there somewhere walking the streets.'

I didn't want to think of the evil that could befall a naïve teenage girl all on her own with no money and with no one to take care of her. I didn't air my thoughts, as Josh was worried enough already. Instead, I tried to be positive and explored the possibility of Emily taking a horse from the stable or begging a ride with some itinerant tradesman, a carter or a carrier, a tinker or even a band of gypsies, but everything I came up with Josh had thought of before.

Suddenly, I had an idea. 'I stopped here because my horse went lame,' I said. 'I'll take one of yours, if I may, and carry on up to the hall.' The more I thought about the idea more I liked it. 'As soon as I get there I'll send Sergeant Finch out to find Emily.'

Josh was not impressed. 'Take a horse from my stable by all means but if you'll forgive me for saying so, Master Thomas, why should Sebastian Finch have any more notion as to where my daughter has gone than I have?'

Sebastian eh? In all the years Finch had worked at the hall I had never known his Christian name.

'I'll tell you why, Josh,' I said with confidence. 'I recently met Sergeant Finch's former commanding officer and in conversation he told me that for a time our head groom served as his provost sergeant and in that capacity he did a remarkably good job. Finding a frightened young girl should be no problem to someone who has successfully tracked down goodness knows how many cunning deserters.'

★ ★ ★

As I expected, Finch was waiting for me at the bridge over the moat. I had also expected the other familiar trappings of homecoming like the bustle of servants and the yapping of dogs but there was none of that, just his solitary figure standing in the snow. I asked him what was going on.

'There have been some changes in the domestic staff, sir,' he said impassively.

'But the dogs, Finch. Where are the dogs?'

He looked at the ground. 'They have been put down, sir.'

'Not Hagar!'

'No, sir. She's up at the stables.'

I was relieved. At least Hagar had been spared but why do away with the rest of the dogs? I asked Finch to explain.

'I understand that it has something to do with Master Cruikshank, sir. They never took to him.'

'My father would never sanction such a thing.'

The old soldier stared straight ahead. 'No, sir, I don't believe he would,' he said.

'For God's sake man. Out with it! We've always been honest with each other haven't we?'

'Well, it's possible Sir Rupert wasn't consulted. You see, sir, Master Cruikshank runs the estate now.'

'He what? Like hell he does!'

I wanted to go and have it out with my

father there and then but it would have to wait. First, I had to get Finch on Emily's trail. We walked to the stable together and I told him as much as I knew. He listened, his weather-beaten face showing genuine concern.

'I'll trot this horse back to Josh Napper's straight away and see what I can dig up, sir,' he said.

'I'm sorry to ask you to do this at Christmas time, Finch.'

There was a glint in his eye that could have been either anger or excitement, or perhaps a touch of both. 'Can you think of a better time to help your neighbour?' he replied.

★   ★   ★

Christmas time! A Yule log blazing away in the hearth, a great bowl of hot mulled wine and a fat goose roasted to perfection. That was what I thought I was coming home to, not to news that Emily had disappeared and Edwin Cruikshank had taken over the estate. What was my father thinking about?

A tall, thin, gaunt faced man dressed in the sober garb of a servant was waiting for me when I got to the hall porch.

'Thomas Neville?' he enquired superciliously.

'*Captain* Thomas Neville, if you please!' I snapped. It was unlike me to be pompous but there was something about this man I didn't take to. 'And who might you be?'

'I am Mandrake, sir, the butler.'

'The devil you are! Where's Norbury?'

He stared straight ahead, focusing his eyes on a point somewhere over my left shoulder. 'I am given to understand, sir, that the previous occupant of this office was discharged.'

'Discharged! Good grief man! Norbury has been butler here for as long as I can remember. What on earth could he possibly have done after all that time to warrant being discharged?'

Mandrake looked away, which I took as a sign that I was to get no more information from him. I was relieved therefore, when at that moment, Giles appeared on the scene, his mischievous smiling face a most welcome sight.

'It's good to see you, Tom,' he said. 'I asked Mandrake here to keep an eye out for you.' He thanked the bony servant and waved him away. 'We expected you earlier, old chap. Getting a bit worried about you and all that.'

'What in God's name is going on here, Giles? The dogs have been put down, there are no servants apart from that sinister fellow and he tells me Norbury has been dismissed.'

'Well, old Norbury always *was* a little too fond of sampling father's port.'

'All butlers drink their master's port! It's one of the perks of the job!'

Giles put a hand on my shoulder and spoke in a reverent whisper as if we were in a Cathedral. 'I'm afraid it's Father who is the problem. Gambling went to his head, you see. It seemed at first he couldn't lose. Money just flowed in. He put the almshouses in hand *and* started work on the tower at St Luke's — he even ordered new bells! It was when Cruikshank went south to attend to some business that the trouble started.'

He moved off down the short passage that led to the great hall. I followed him closely; anxious to hear what was coming next.

He continued to speak in a hushed voice. 'Rather than wait for him to return, Father bet on anything and everything. He'd somehow got it into his head he had the Midas touch but without Cruikshank's expert guidance he lost of course. And the more he lost the more frantic his betting became, doubling up, trying to recoup — you know the sort of thing. He was drinking a lot of brandy by this time and the worse things became, the more he drank. Eventually, a lot of the servants had to go because we hadn't the money to pay them, the work on the almshouses ground to a halt and the estate started to go downhill. I did what I could, but without money I couldn't halt the decline. We were on the verge of disaster when Edwin Cruikshank came back. He's a wonderful man, Tom. He's completely justified Mamma's confidence in him. Since he took charge everything is fine. He even bought some land from us so that we could pay off our creditors.'

I could hardly believe what I was hearing. 'We've sold Neville land?'

'Just the old priory.'

'But that's within sight of the house!'

'There was no alternative, old chum. I know it's your inheritance and all that, but bills have to be paid.'

With everything that had gone before, the scene that met my eyes as we entered the great hall was quite unexpected. A Yule log was burning in the hearth, a huge monster that must have taken a team of horses to get it up to the house, and a gang of men to manhandle it into the fireplace. There it blazed merrily with an occasional crackle sending a shower of sparks up the great black maw of the chimney. Its flickering flames were reflected back in the big silver bowl on the long table from which my mother was ladling a steaming liquid into little silver cups. So, we've got the mulled wine as well! It was just like Christmas had always been except Mother was different somehow, younger looking and wearing a dress in a flimsy transparent material instead of her usual, more practical clothing. And standing in my father's place in front of the fireplace, with one arrogant booted foot on the hearthstone was Edwin Cruikshank.

'Ah, Thomas!' he shouted. 'Come on in, my boy. A bit late aren't you?'

My mother looked up with a wan smile. She seemed to be in a world of her own.

I stayed where I was. 'I would like to see my father if it please you, sir,' I said.

'Certainly, certainly. But your ride from Chester must have been gruelling, you will want to go to your room first surely?' He snapped his fingers and Mandrake stepped out of the shadows. 'Take Master Thomas' bags to his room and see he has hot water and towels.'

Giles stepped forward. 'I've got to go to St Luke's now, I'm afraid,' he said, pulling a face. 'Christmas Eve and all that . . . It's good to have you home again, Tom.' He waved to the others in the room and left.

I changed out of my regimentals, putting on some old, familiar and altogether more comfortable, country clothes and went over to the east wing, making straight for my father's room. Inside, the air smelt stale and it was very cold for there was no fire in the grate. My father was lying in bed with the covers pulled up under his chin. His face was ashen and his eyes ringed with dark shadows. I could detect no sign of movement and for a terrible moment I thought he'd passed away. There was a small phial on the table by the bed. I picked it up and removed the stopper.

'For God's sake don't drink that! Unless you want to sleep like the dead for the next twelve hours.'

It was my father who had spoken. His eyes were open but he made no attempt to sit up.

'Old spindleshanks thought I'd taken it but I fooled him. I held it in my mouth until he'd gone, then I spat it into the chamber pot.' He laughed feebly. 'I'm sorry you see me in such a condition, Thomas. The drink is a terrible thing. I awake in the early hours vowing I'll never touch another drop and then when morning comes I'm so depressed I just have to have one to put myself on an even keel and then, well, that's it isn't it?' He reached out and grabbed my wrist. 'Take over the estate, Thomas, please, for me,' he said, his red-rimmed eyes pleading. 'God forbid that control of it should ever leave the family.'

'So, Sir Rupert, you are awake.'

Cruikshank must have come up the servants' stairs. His sudden appearance startled me and I felt guilty at being discovered here, which was nonsense of course, for why shouldn't I be in my own father's bedroom? I was suddenly conscious that I was still holding the phial in my hand.

'This is an odd looking bottle. Did Doctor Ramsay prescribe this?' I said, perhaps a little too casually.

Cruikshank laughed. He really was the most engaging of men and I felt strangely at ease in his company. He may be somewhat larger than life and annoyingly overconfident, but is it his fault if the ladies find him so attractive? I would count myself fortunate to be so blessed.

'Doctors?' he said. 'Why bother with doctors when all that's wrong with your father is a surfeit of brandy.' He took the phial from me. 'He doesn't need some old fool with a jar of leeches, all he needs is rest,' adding with a knowing wink, 'and a little hair of the dog.'

I looked down at the corpse-like body in the bed and whispered, 'But he looks awful. Is he eating anything?'

Cruikshank put a friendly arm around my

shoulders and I found myself being led out of the room.

'Thomas,' he said softly, squeezing my shoulder with his hand like some benevolent uncle. 'If you had seen your father as he was when I got back from my trip south you would be thanking your lucky stars to find him so composed. I went away leaving a sane, intelligent and compassionate gentleman only to come back to find him replaced by an aggressive and violent wild-man.'

Mandrake appeared with a tray covered by a white linen cloth. We stood aside to allow him access to my father's room. The tray passed a few inches from my nose and I recognised the smell of hot chicken broth. Cruikshank nodded approvingly.

'The longer Sir Rupert sleeps the less he drinks,' he continued, 'and when he is awake he is sufficiently docile to allow us to give him nourishment, to exercise him and allow him to fulfil his bodily functions. Trust me, my man and I have done this before.'

It all sounded very logical and if I had listened to that soothing, velvety voice much longer I am sure I would have agreed with him. Giles said father's drinking had got worse and Cruikshank seemed to know what he was doing. Nevertheless, I wasn't happy to leave my father's fate completely in the hands

106

of a stranger, however persuasive and experienced they may claim to be.

'I would still like Doctor Ramsay to see my father, if it's all the same to you,' I said.

Cruikshank didn't seem the least put out by this suggestion. 'Of course!' he said, with an enchanting smile. 'If that is your wish I'll have the good doctor sent for straight away.' He went to go back into my father's room but hesitated at the door. 'I do have your mother's complete confidence in this matter,' he said, 'and whilst I do not object to you asking for a second opinion you would do better to save your money, for whatever the sawbones may say, the treatment will not change.'

The smile was still on his face but his strange eyes sent a shiver down my spine. He went back into my father's room and closed the door, the snap of the latch putting a full stop to our conversation.

Suddenly, there was a commotion at the bottom of the servants' stairs and Sergeant Finch called, 'Master Thomas! Master Thomas!'

'Up here!' I shouted.

There was a clatter of boots on the stairs and Finch appeared, very much out of breath. 'Best come quick, Master Thomas,' he gasped. 'I know where she's gone. Josh is downstairs with fresh horses. They've taken her to Liverpool. Emily's being shipped off in a slaver!'

As much as I hated leaving my father to the tender mercies of Edwin Cruikshank and his sinister servant, if Emily was about to be put on a slave ship there was no time to lose, we had to leave for Liverpool right away. I ran back to my room, grabbed an old hat and my long riding coat and joined Finch and Napper in the yard. They were already mounted, their high-spirited horses snorting and scraping at the cobbles impatiently with their fore hooves. Finch was holding the reins of a third horse which was saddled up for me.

Much to Josh's annoyance we set off at a canter. Having never been much of a horseman, he was all for galloping off at full speed to find his daughter but it was a good many miles to Liverpool and there was nothing to be gained by punishing our mounts in a mad dash only to have them drop with exhaustion before we got there. He accepted my reasoning readily enough when he had it explained to him. As we jogged along I asked Sergeant Finch to tell me what he had found out.

'It was old Simon who put me on to it,' he said, his weather-beaten face split by a wide grin. 'Rushford's coach was in the yard when I got there and he told me it had been there when young Emily went missing so I took a chance and went across to Welsh Meg's, and tally-ho! There was the gentleman's coachman.'

Josh took up the story, the jowls on his fat face bouncing up and down in rhythm with the horse. 'Sebastian brought the man back to my place and after a bit of gentle persuasion he confessed to having taken Emily to Liverpool.'

'On instructions from Cruikshank!' Finch added. 'They'd had a row, remember? The coachman was even able to tell us what they'd rowed about! Emily is pregnant with Cruikshank's child!'

The news was a hammer blow and it was all I could do not to throw caution to the wind and spur my horse into a gallop. I glanced at Josh. He was crying unashamedly but still following my instructions and jogging along at my side, so I held myself in check.

'As Emily is a mulatto,' Finch continued, shooting a furtive glance at Josh, 'Cruikshank gave this man some money and the name of someone in Liverpool who could place her on one of the slave ships going to the Carolinas or the West Indies. Neat eh? Problem solved!' He spat in the road. 'The Liverpool man goes by the name of Wheeler and hangs out on the waterfront.'

It was dark by the time we reached the town on the north bank of the Mersey estuary. Liverpool was a rapidly expanding seaport, second only on the English west coast to Bristol. By day it was a bustling and busy place and at night it was noisy and lively, its inhabitants being more open-minded and liberal than the reserved and thrifty folk of nearby Manchester.

Leaving our horses at a livery stable we made our way on foot through the warren of narrow streets at the dockside. After we had been to three establishments without success I felt our search was taking too long and suggested we split up.

I had just made my first solo forage into yet another noisy hostelry when all hell broke loose. Women screamed and there was a sudden mad scramble with people running in all directions, smashing chairs and tables in their panic. I then saw the reason for this alarm. Several large sailors from His Majesty's navy, armed with long, wooden, belaying pins, entered the establishment, forming a tight cluster around the doorway. There followed a moment of weighted silence, broken only by one of the women quietly sobbing in a corner. Then the sailors parted and a young Midshipman entered the room.

'I am looking for seamen to serve aboard

one of His Majesty's ships,' he said in a high-pitched, adolescent voice. 'Do I have any volunteers?' There wasn't a sound other than the woman's continual sobbing. 'All right bo'sun,' he said. 'Do your duty.'

Then it was pandemonium, with the sailors wading into the crowd and grabbing any man who looked reasonably young and fit.

A big fellow loomed up in front of me. 'Here's a likely lad,' he roared.

I fended him off but another joined in.

'You can't take me, God damn it!' I shouted. 'I'm not a seaman, I'm a gentleman.'

Someone grabbed my sleeve; I struggled to get free.

And then the lights went out.

6

While I was relating my story, Clive took great delight in amazing us with a seemingly endless array of deliciously interesting and highly spiced dishes that culminated in the sweetest of sweetmeats served by two, shy, young native girls who, my host informed me with a laugh, were not on the menu.

The only femininity in my life in past months had been the scabby, gin-soaked harridans that were rowed out to the *Indefatigable* whenever we hit port. These delicate Indian girls were little more than children and their dark skin reminded me painfully of Emily. I surprised one by offering *her* a sweetmeat and after a glance at Clive, who gave permission with a nod of his head, she had taken the treat, rewarding me with a most beautiful smile.

As the first light of day began to appear in the sky I was intrigued to see Tobias produce a timepiece. It was gold and the size of a large round snuffbox. I'd noticed the fob earlier protruding from his waistcoat pocket and wondered if it was in fact attached to one of these newfangled watches, as they were being called.

The action was not lost on Clive either. 'Can I see that?' he asked, holding out his hand.

Tobias gave it to him. The great man's eyes lit up and he played with it like a child, snapping open the lid that covered the face and snapping it shut again. 'I really must get one of these,' he said.

Their talk of coiled spring drives and balance-spring regulators had me completely lost, and like Clive, I envied Tobias, but the price of one of these modern miracles was well beyond the means of a subaltern in a county regiment.

Clive handed the fob watch back to Tobias. He turned to me and said, 'I'm glad you came to me, Neville. By the sound of things you are desperately needed in England. Don't worry I'll get you there.'

I had not misjudged him. He was still the Robert Clive I remembered. I was both relieved and excited. 'There's an East Indiaman in the harbour now,' I said eagerly.

He held up a hand. 'Whoa! Slow down! You, sir, are a deserter from His Majesty's navy and take it from me they will be looking for you . . . and they will be keeping a close watch on that ship, particularly as she's due to sail for London in a few days. I'm sorry old

Neville, but you're stuck here until the Royal Navy leaves Madras.'

The thought of kicking my heels in a foreign land for goodness knows how long was depressing. I had no money for God's sake! How was I going to support myself? There was no doubt I could stay on here as Clive's guest, he evidently enjoyed having people around him to show off to, but it is not in my nature to be a sponger.

Tobias saw my jaw drop. 'If you want to send a letter home, I can ask the East Indiaman's captain to take it for you,' he said accommodatingly.

My heart leaped at the thought of being able to contact England. 'My regiment probably listed me as a deserter months ago so I'd be grateful if you can get a message to my colonel,' I said, knowing that my uncle would immediately inform my parents of my situation.

'That's it!' Clive shouted, his eyes shining. 'That's what we'll do with you.'

I was puzzled by this sudden outburst and I suppose it showed.

'Fix you up with a job, old Neville. Something to stop you fretting until we can get you back to England.'

Employment brought pay and pay brought independence. I was all for that. 'What had you in mind, sir?' I asked.

He chuckled. 'Something that will make good use of your training, and somewhere the Royal Navy will never think to look for you.' He stood savouring the moment, a huge grin on his face. 'You, old Neville, are going to join the East India Company Militia!'

★ ★ ★

After a bath and a shave I reported as instructed to Clive's rooms where I found him putting together a uniform from what, to me, seemed a vast wardrobe of military clothing. He was in very high spirits.

'Try this on,' he said, holding a coat against me for size. 'We are much the same in height although you're a bit on the skinny side.'

The garment was lined with the finest silk. He was right about it being a little generous in width but by the way it sat on my shoulders I could tell it had been expertly tailored. It felt good on and appeared to have hardly been worn, yet its colour was badly faded by the sun. It bore the insignia of a lieutenant.

'Yes, that should do nicely,' he said. 'We don't want anything that looks too new. Can't have the men thinking you're a novice, what? And you'll have to put up with the drop in rank I'm afraid. I am not without influence in the militia but there are no vacancies in the Madras garrison for captains.'

Some time later that morning he took me to meet the Garrison Commander, Major James Fraser, a small, peppery Scotsman. I was wearing the brown coat, as it was not thought prudent for me to wear my new uniform yet.

The major greeted Clive as if he were royalty. He ushered us into his quarters, sat us down and produced a bottle of whisky and some glasses.

'Who is this you've brought with you, Robert?' he asked, eyeing me suspiciously.

Clive drew himself up and said proudly, 'This, James, is Thomas Neville, late of His Majesty's twenty-second of foot. He's looking for a position until he can get a passage back to England.'

The major regarded me appraisingly. 'The Cheshires eh?' he said. 'Were you at Dettingen, laddie?' I nodded with a smug grin but immediately regretted it when the little officer glared at me witheringly and growled, 'Your regiment did us Scots no favours when you saved King George's life!'

'Come on, James, you old Jacobite,' Clive said with a laugh. 'The Cheshires fought valiantly at Dettingen and you would have been the first to come to the aid of your commander-in-chief had you seen the enemy's cavalry bearing down on him.'

The major splashed whisky into three glasses. 'Och! I suppose I would at that,' he said grudgingly. 'And I'm needing experienced officers . . . as well you know, Robert, you conniving bastard!'

Clive put a friendly hand on the major's shoulder. 'Then seize this opportunity! The lad's got the right spirit. I know, we have fought side by side.' He winked at me. 'Or perhaps I should say, back to back, eh, Neville?'

With the hero of Arcot as my sponsor, there was no doubting Fraser would take me on his staff, and later that day I stood, with Clive at my side, on the fort's small parade square as the major introduced me to the officers and men of his command.

I had changed into uniform for the occasion and I felt rather grand, and I believe I looked it too, even though I do say so myself. My generous host had sent for a tailor to make the slight alteration needed to the coat and while that was being done he took me on a shopping expedition to kit me out with the various personal items I would need for my short stay in India. He even helped me to carry the purchases across to the room that had been allocated to me in the Fort.

As I stood there, on parade, listening with some embarrassment to the major delivering his eulogy, I searched the ranks for the two soldiers I had met after jumping ship. The big one, Daniel Coggins, was easy to spot. I looked for some sign of recognition but there was none. He stood at the end of the line; ramrod straight, his big red face impassive, his eyes looking straight ahead. It was a while before I picked out his compatriot, Archie Fowler. The smaller man was in the middle of the second rank, and he was watching me. Was that a puzzled look on his pointed face? Did he recognise me? I decided it unlikely he would associate a well turned out army officer with the scruffy, bearded seaman I had been but a short time before, but I would be on my guard nevertheless.

Major Fraser's way of getting as much value from my services as he could in a short time was to make me his training officer and I spent the next few days putting the men through their drill. They were certainly not the smartest soldiers I have ever seen on parade but there was nothing I could teach them about forming three ranks or loading and firing a musket. What I did introduce them to was volley firing, a most effective way of concentrating small arms firepower, and my speciality, speed-marching. Those who had seen action, and they were the majority, immediately recognised the benefits of both disciplines and were eager to practice them.

I had been at the garrison just a few days short of a month when I received a summons from the major to report to his headquarters. It was just after midday so I knew it must be something of importance otherwise James Fraser, like every other European in Madras, would be stretched out in the shade somewhere.

On my way there, and in order to take advantage of what little breeze there was, I walked along the ramparts of the Fort. The *Indefatigable* had sailed long since and the only big ship left in the harbour was an armed merchantman flying French colours. For a thousandth time I searched the horizon, there was no East Indiaman, nothing.

When I got to the major's office I found him attempting to calm a group of irate Indian merchants. He rolled his eyes at me as I came in.

'I can really do without this!' he said, in an aside through teeth gritted into a false smile. Then, for the benefit of the delegation, he announced loudly in his very best diplomatic voice, 'We have a very serious problem here,

Lieutenant. A young girl has been abducted from the colony by agents of Suraja Dowla.'

'Suraja . . . ?' I queried, having lost the rest of the name.

'Wake up you idle bastard!' he shouted.

The little major mopped his brow with a limp handkerchief and I realised, with some relief, that this outburst was directed not at me but at the *punkahwallah*, the small boy whose job it was to keep the fan in the ceiling moving. The lad had dozed off but at Fraser's bark he shot upright and began heaving with all his might on the cord. The big fabric-covered frame began to waft backwards and forwards once again, stirring the heavy air in an impression of a breeze.

'Suraja Dowla,' he said, 'is the Nawab of Bengal. A young man with more money and power than is good for him . . . This is Devraj Rawal,' he said indicating a richly dressed Indian at the centre of the group. 'He moved his family here from Calcutta when it became obvious to him that the Nawab had designs on his daughter.'

I was puzzled. Why should this merchant object to his daughter being courted by a wealthy young prince?

'I thought it was every father's dream that his daughter should make a good marriage,' I ventured.

The Indian replied in heavily accented but otherwise excellent English. 'That monster has no thought of marriage, Lieutenant *sahib*,' he said, solemnly. 'Suraja Dowla is an evil man who slits open pregnant women's bellies out of idle curiosity and sinks ferryboats just to study the behaviour of people who are drowning. If he takes a liking to someone's daughter — or to their son for that matter, and he doesn't mind either way — it is purely to satisfy his sadistic pleasure. I would rather my daughter were dead than with that wicked man.'

The merchants began jabbering excitedly among themselves again. Fraser cleared his throat and produced a silver snuffbox from his waistcoat pocket. With great ceremony he proceeded to pinch a quantity of the fine powder between finger and thumb and tap off the excess on the edge of the open box.

'We must try to get this child back, laddie,' he whispered before sniffing noisily. 'At least we must be seen to be trying. These natives who trade with us expect our protection and Rawal's a powerful figure among them. If we do nothing about this abduction, like as not they'll go over to the French, and the East India Company in Madras might as well shut up shop and go home.'

'How much of a start have they got?' I said.

'About an hour, and I'm afraid with that damned Frenchman in the harbour I can only spare you a patrol.'

He walked with me to the door and as I left he shouted after me, loudly so the merchants should hear, 'Make a thorough search, Lieutenant! Leave no stone unturned!'

A patrol could be anything from six to ten men, plus NCOs and officers. I had no idea how many were in the abduction party but I could move more quickly with a small group, and speed was of the essence. I ran to the barracks and grabbed the first man I saw, an old campaigner by the look of him sitting in the shade of the portico, in his shirtsleeves, smoking a pipe. I called to him and he hurriedly got to his feet.

'Ten men, muskets, ammunition pouches, water bottles, on parade here in five minutes, right?'

He could see I was in no mood to discuss the matter. 'Yes, sir!' he shouted in reply and disappeared inside calling out names as he went.

I ran back to my room, yelling to my servant to fill my water bottle whilst stuffing a brace of pistols in the capacious pockets of my coat and buckling on my sabre. When I got back to the barrack square, ten soldiers were lined up in two ranks in column of route ready to march off, half of them were Indian *sepoys* under the command of a fiercely moustachioed *sirdar*, a native NCO.

I had come across this man before. He had previously worked for the French and I didn't feel comfortable with him, possibly because he had changed sides. But he was an experienced NCO and I needed someone to look after the natives, so I let him stay.

My two old friends were among the Europeans on parade, and this I found comforting in a strange sort of way.

The man I had ordered to assemble the patrol stepped forward and touched a knuckle to his forehead. Now that he was properly dressed, his badges of rank proclaimed him to be a warrant officer.

'Ten men in full marching order, sir!' he barked and then, in a more conversational tone, he added, 'I thought you might be needing an English NCO on this patrol, Lieutenant, so I've taken the liberty of kitting myself out to come with you.'

That made thirteen on parade but I liked this man. He was older than the rest and that meant experience. By the way he carried himself he had seen service in the regular army. He certainly seemed very capable.

'I'll be very pleased to have you with us . . . Sergeant Major?'

'Company Sergeant Major William Hatton, sir. Late of the Royal Welch Fusiliers.'

My thoughts went racing back to big Owen, my guide and protector through those tough days on the *Indefatigable*, and without thinking I said, and rather rudely when I think about it, 'But you're not Welsh!'

'I'm a Shropshire lad, sir, born and bred,' he answered proudly, 'from Ludlow — that's where the Royal Welch was formed, sir, Ludlow, by Lord Herbert in sixteen eighty-nine — and he was an Englishman too, sir.' He lowered his voice. 'The Company has seen fit to retire me, sir, so I'm on the next boat back to England. This will be my last chance to see a bit of action.'

I felt that I couldn't ask for a better second-in-command for this expedition. 'Face the men to the front and stand them at ease for briefing, Master Hatton,' I said with a grin.

It took but a few moments to explain our mission to the patrol. I noted a flicker of fear in the eyes of the Indian soldiers at the mention of Suraja Dowla although the face of their *sirdar* remained as inscrutable as that of the big, scar-faced veteran of Arcot.

Major Fraser's well-to-do Indian merchants stood outside the Headquarters building to watch us go by. I called for a smart 'eyes left' as we marched past them, which we did in the best parade ground fashion. Once clear of the fort I gave the order to tail arms and break step and we settled down to the easy loping pace that the men had practiced many times before. This was new to CSM Hatton but he soon fell into the rhythm. He smiled and nodded to indicate his approval.

We went north. Suraja Dowla's agents would need a boat to take their captive back to Bengal and the best place to hide such a vessel would be in the ruins of the old Portuguese settlement north of the fort. This long-abandoned site was gradually being reclaimed by the jungle and was now almost hidden in a forest of interwoven creepers and vines. The *sirdar* volunteered to go on ahead with a machete to clear a way through for us. We arrived on a grassy plateau overlooking a small bay that was well out of sight of the fort, and there it was, a lateen-rigged, two-masted dhow. I was well pleased with this early success and in no way did I foresee the disaster that was about to follow.

I signalled to the patrol to stay back and, taking the two NCO's with me, I advanced carefully to the rim of the plateau. The dhow was riding at anchor. It appeared to be deserted. Suddenly, the *sirdar* let out a piercing yell and from the surrounding undergrowth dozens of screaming, sword-waving pirates fell upon us. A blow from the treacherous Indian's machete felled Hatton to the ground. I drew my sabre but with no room to use it effectively I was quickly overpowered by sheer weight of numbers. My last memory before one of the brigands knocked me senseless was the sight of the patrol drawn up in two ranks, volley firing into the screaming hoard with commendable discipline and to great effect.

I awoke. The only light was that which filtered in through the uneven gaps between a door and its frame but it was enough for me to make out a ceiling and walls made of rough wooden planking and a floor that was littered with foul smelling straw. A rat scuttled past and I was grateful to be lying on a bunk above the filth. I had a terrible feeling of *déjà vu*. I was back on a ship. Of course! The dhow! The pirates had taken me prisoner, but for what reason? Then I thought of Suraja Dowla's idea of sport and wished that I hadn't.

I sat up and the rattle of chains broke the silence. The movement restored my circulation. Feeling came flooding back into my flesh and with it a sharp burning soreness at my wrists and ankles where rough iron cuffs had chafed the skin. I cursed loudly. The sudden pain had made me break out in a sweat and this was now trickling like ice water down the hollow of my back I shivered and realised then that I was naked.

My situation looked hopeless and I began to despair. Then, for some inexplicable reason the holy man, Hari Lal, came to mind and I could hear his voice, speaking softy to me in that hypnotic, singsong, way of his.

'*You must make for yourself a happy place in your head, Neville sahib, where you can go to find peace and renew your strength.*'

Suddenly, it was as if I was lying in a lush, sunny meadow in Cheshire watching my foolish nag with his head through the fence, trying to reach the grass on the other side and I realised I was smiling. Here I was, lying in chains in the stinking brig of a pirate dhow, facing goodness knows what horrors and I was actually smiling! That awful feeling of desperation had left me. In its place was an angry determination to get myself out of this mess and I said a silent word of thanks to that strange little man with the beaky nose.

The door of the brig opened and several grinning, bearded cutthroats jostled each other to get a look at me. Then their excited pointing and jabbering stopped as suddenly as it had started and they reverently moved aside to admit another of their number who, by his arrogant bearing I took to be their leader. His clothing was as filthy and ragged as that of his crew but the pair of jewel-encrusted pistols protruding ostentatiously from a greasy cummerbund and a magnificent sapphire the size of a musket ball pinned like a third eye in the centre of his turban testified to his success as a pirate captain.

His face was as brown and shiny as a chestnut and his eyes small and dark. Unlike the rest of his band he was beardless but sported the longest drooping moustache I had ever seen. He looked at me for a long time without speaking, a gloating smile hovering about his thin cruel lips.

'*Monsieur Lieutenant,*' he said, giving me a mocking salute. He then spat on the floor. His audience took this as a signal for them to laugh and jeer and make catcalls, which they did with great enthusiasm until he held up his hand for silence. He then proceeded to talk to me in very bad French. It was possibly his only European language but he knew that his ability to converse with a foreigner on what appeared to be equal terms was immensely impressive to his illiterate crew. I could just about make out his meaning.

'You come here to snatch the girl, but we

snatch you, eh?' he said.

I was surprised to hear one of the men quietly translating this which, when he had finished, was followed by another round of raucous laughter. The captain grinned and nodded to his crew, basking in their applause for a moment before holding up his hand again.

'The Nawab have great passion for the girl, he give plenty money for her. You are friend of Robert Clive, I think Robert Clive give plenty money for you, eh?'

The captain waited for this to be translated and for the cheers of approval that followed.

'Your men, they are all dead except for this fellow, eh?' He reached behind him and drew forward the traitorous *sirdar*. I realised then who his interpreter had been. 'This man will go back to the fort and tell Robert Clive you are my prisoner and we sail for Bengal on the tide. I send you ashore alive at Fort William in return for plenty money from Robert Clive, eh?'

The captain and his followers then left and the door of the brig slammed shut behind them, plunging me into semidarkness once more. Their voices faded into the distance leaving me with the sound of the waves slapping on the side of the boat and the noise of the rats scurrying across the floor.

I searched my shackles, the padlocks and even the bolts securing them to the bulkhead for some sign of weakness, something I could work on to get myself free. It took me a long time in the dark to feel around each link, each hasp, loop and pin in the metalwork but it got me nowhere. In a fit of frustration I slammed the manacles on my wrists against the wooden bunk, which was a foolish thing to do for all I achieved was the addition of more painful abrasions to my already tortured flesh. I lay back panting with anger, trying desperately hard to imagine myself back in that sunlit Cheshire meadow.

There was the sound of keys in the door. It seemed hours since the captain's visit. Had he returned for more gloating? God! I hope he's brought some water.

'Quietly does it, sir,' an English voice whispered. The door opened just wide enough to allow a figure to slip into the room before it was closed again and locked from the inside. 'Right,' he said. He was closer now and fumbling for the padlocks. 'Let's see which key fits these.'

'Master Hatton!' I exclaimed. 'By all that's holy, what are you doing here?'

He quickly had my throbbing wrists free and began working on my ankles.

'That damned traitor knocked me cold,' he

whispered. 'When I came to there wasn't a living soul to be seen on that plateau.'

'They told me all the patrol were dead,' I said miserably.

'Ah well, they were wrong there, sir. The lads put up a good show. With you and me *hors de combat* so to speak, Private Coggins took command and they made a tactical withdrawal into the ruins, volley firing all the way. They took some casualties but they accounted for a good many of the enemy.'

My spirits rose even higher with that good news. 'What's our present state?' I asked.

'Six fit for active duty, sir, four Europeans and two *sepoys*. There's one European and two *sepoy* walking wounded. I sent them back to the fort.'

My ankles were free now and I tried standing up. I was a bit wobbly and had to grab hold of the bulkhead to steady myself.

'God! That feels good,' I said.

'Take it easy, sir. No need to rush things. I've got my water bottle here. You sit for a moment and have a drink.'

I took the flask from him gratefully. 'How many of you are here on the ship?' I asked.

The water was warm and brackish but at that moment it tasted better than the finest Champagne.

The CSM was back at the door, unlocking

it. He opened it a crack and peered out. In the dim light I could see there was something odd about his outline. I then realised what it was, he was dressed as a native.

'Five sir, counting myself. I left the *sepoys* on the beach. With you gone, sir, we were wondering what to do next when we saw the *sirdar* being rowed ashore. When they landed we jumped them, changed clothes with the pirates and rowed the double-crossing bastard back to the ship again. I must say their lookouts are very lackadaisical. They wouldn't do in my company. We relieved them of their posts.'

Although I couldn't see his face I knew he was smiling. There was a loud scraping noise that my experience at sea told me was the sound of hatch covers being replaced.

'All secure, sir,' came from the other side of the door. Hatton opened it and there, peering in, his little pointed face split ear to ear with a wide grin, was Archie Fowler. 'Everyone who wasn't on watch is locked in the forward hold, Master Hatton,' he reported.

'And those *on* watch?' Hatton enquired.

The little man's face took on a wicked smile. 'Let's say they won't cause us no more bother, sir.' Then he saw me. 'God bless you, Master Neville!' he exclaimed, pronouncing 'God' as 'Gawd'. He disappeared for a few moments and returned with a bundle of clothing.

'You'd best put something on, sir, or you'll catch your death.'

He handed me a rough homespun shirt and a *dhoti*. Both garments had an unpleasant sour smell and were heavily bloodstained.

'It's all right, sir, the bloke I got them off won't be needing them anymore,' he said.

I was suddenly conscious of my nakedness. I could hardly command a boarding party in my birthday suit so the stinking rags Fowler was offering would have to do until I could find something better. I took them and put them on.

'Have you found the girl?' I asked.

Fowler looked sheepish. 'Well, we have and we haven't, if you know what I mean? Aint that so Master Hatton?'

Hatton stepped forward smartly. He looked a bit ridiculous standing to attention dressed in pirate's clothes but to the Company Sergeant Major there was only one way to make a report to a senior officer, even one wearing a bloodstained shirt and a loincloth.

'What Private Fowler is trying to say, sir, is that the girl is in the captain's cabin, and he is threatening to kill her if we don't leave his boat.'

'My mate, Dan, er, Private Coggins, is up there now, sir,' Fowler said. 'He's got the *sirdar* with him. The captain don't speak no English, so the Indian is translating what Dan says into his lingo.' I didn't like the sound of that and it must have shown on my face for he added, 'Don't worry, sir. Dan's got the business end of his bayonet at the Indian's throat. He won't cross us again.'

The little soldier led the way to the captain's cabin where we found things exactly as he had described them. I could see what Hatton meant about the lookouts, you could have dressed Dan Coggins as the Great Mogul himself and he would still look like an English soldier. The nervous tic was playing on his face again making his sinister leer even more chilling. There was nothing enigmatic about the *sirdar's* expression on this occasion. His hands were tied and his eyes bulged with terror as Coggins held him by the hair with one hand and with the other pricked the skin beneath his chin with the point of a bayonet.

'We have your ship, Captain,' I called out in French. 'I ask you to surrender.'

'*Monsieur Lieutenant!* So, you are a free man, eh? You tell your men to go, yes? They leave my ship or the girl is dead!'

He must have twisted her arm or something as I heard a squeal from the other side of the ill-fitting door. A plan was beginning to form in my mind.

'Fowler, go back to the brig and bring back as much of the straw that's on the floor as you can. Hurry now!'

He wasn't gone long before he was back with an armful of the filthy muck. Much of it was damp but mercifully I did manage to tease out some dry stuff, which I placed at the bottom of the door.

'Let me have your pistol Master Hatton,' I whispered. Then, in a loud voice and in my best schoolboy French I said, 'Listen to me very carefully, Captain. The girl's father would rather his daughter be dead than with Suraja Dowla — and you know why. We *will* leave your ship but we will leave it in flames!'

I fired the pistol into the dry straw and the flash of the lock set it alight. I began piling the damp stuff on top and Hatton, quickly realising what I was doing, joined in. Great clouds of smoke issued from the smouldering heap and very soon there was the sound of coughing from within the cabin and the rattle of a key in the lock. The door burst open and the hostage tumbled out with the pirate captain close behind her, his eyes streaming and his pistols levelled. I read the look on his face and flung myself at the girl just as he discharged one of the pistols. Fortunately, the

135

impetus of my leap carried us both out of the line of fire. As we fell I caught a glimpse of Fowler drawing a pistol from his belt.

'Don't shoot him!' I shouted.

The captain half turned towards me and was immediately felled by a mighty blow from Dan Coggins's fist. I got to my feet. The *sirdar* lay on the deck bleeding profusely. He had been hit by the ball from the captain's pistol and was mortally wounded. The little Indian girl was wide-eyed and trembling with fear. I tried to reassure her but strangely enough it was Coggins she took to. He knew a few words of her language and there was something about the big ugly soldier that she found comforting. Whatever it was beat me, but I was pleased that one of our party was able to calm her down and let her know we meant her no harm.

'The prisoner is all secure, sir, and ready to move off.' It was Hatton. I turned to see the pirate captain, his wrists securely tied, held firmly in the CSM's grip.

I was puzzled. 'I don't want any prisoners, Master Hatton.'

'But you stopped Private Fowler from shooting him?'

'Only because the villain is wearing my coat! For goodness sake, take it off him and lock him in the hold with the others.'

I found more of my uniform in the captain's cabin so I was able to return to shore reasonably presentable. The others changed back into the clothing they had left on the beach and we set off for the fort in good order as well as in good spirits.

7

The wounded had already told the story, so when our party marched through the gates, the whole garrison turned out to welcome us, Major Fraser and his staff spilling out into the road from the Officers' Mess and cheering as loudly as the men.

Without any word from me, each one of that battered little group squared his shoulders and got into step. I had put CSM Hatton in command and I marched with the men. They were professional soldiers all, and I was proud to be one of them. Thinking about it, it was probably just as well they *were* soldiers; otherwise they would probably be in prison somewhere, or worse. Little Archie Fowler for instance was still wearing the sapphire studded turban he had taken from the pirate captain and Dan Coggins had the jewelled pistols stuck in his belt.

The big scar-faced man had impressed me on this patrol and I was all set to recommend him for promotion until I voiced my intentions to the CSM on the beach.

'He's a good soldier, sir,' he said. 'He's respected by his mates and he likes that. If you promote him they won't trust him anymore and that would make him a lonely and unhappy man. If you want my opinion, sir, he's best left as he is.'

We halted on the parade square where it seemed all the traders and merchants in Madras were assembled. I spotted the two men I had met with Tobias Bloom in Charles Street. On this occasion the fat, red-faced man was all smiles and the thin, elegant one was waving his silver topped cane enthusiastically and shouting, 'Hoorah!'

Devraj Rawal was there, of course, along with his entourage, and as soon as he saw his daughter he let out a loud shout and ran forward to snatch her from the arms of the big soldier. After almost squeezing all the breath out of the child, the Indian held her from him at arms length with a fearful look in his eyes.

'She is quite unharmed,' I said.

He turned to me; his face wet with tears. 'You have brought back my happiness, Lieutenant *sahib*,' he said quietly.

When I told Hatton to dismiss the patrol, the rest of the fort's 'brutal and licentious soldiery' ran forward and flocked around us, cheering and thumping us on the back unmercifully. Some of them hoisted Archie Fowler up on their shoulders and they would have done the same with the CSM had he not good-naturedly reminded them of the dignity of his rank.

I had reached the point where I could take no more of this boisterous adulation. My wrists were sore, blood was seeping through my leggings and I smelled like an abattoir. All I wanted to do was to get back to my quarters and soak for a long time in a hot bath, and afterwards apply some soothing ointment to my abrasions. I looked for the surgeon and saw him on the periphery of the crowd with the English traders. As I was squeezing my way through to him a hand grabbed my arm.

'Just a moment, old Neville.' It was Clive. There was a twinkle in his eye. 'The *Admiral Vernon* arrived this morning,' he said. 'She returns to England in two weeks, I've booked a passage on her — for both of us.'

I received this news with mixed feelings. My objective for so long had simply been to get back home so I was delighted to know that I was finally to be on my way, but in order to retain my sanity during those awful early days on the *Indefatigable* I had concocted a scenario in which Josh Napper had found his daughter and had taken her home. I had hidden behind this fairy tale for a long time; I was now going to have to face up to the truth.

But what was that Clive said? He'd booked a passage for *both* of us? I asked him to explain.

'I thought you would appreciate some company,' he said with a grin. He steered me away from the crowd, his face taking on a more serious look. 'India is a country of spiritual wisdom, of material splendour, of gentleness of manners and benevolent dispositions but I've had enough of it. I haven't seen my family for ten years. I've made my fortune and now I want to go home.'

So, the 'victor of Arcot' was actually confessing to feeling homesick. I had no doubt that he was a rich man. All the suppliers to the settlement paid the steward a commission on their sales and with the Company paying a victualling allowance for every soldier in the garrison, the commissary could make a good profit by buying their provisions cheaply, and Clive was known to be a tough bargainer. It was said that he had amassed enough money to set himself up as a substantial country landowner back in England. I asked him if that was his intention.

That put the smile back on his face. 'My dear old Neville,' he said. 'I'm not one for sitting around twiddling my thumbs; I shall go into politics. Who knows, perhaps one day I'll be Prime Minister.'

Clive had one more surprise up his sleeve. He told me he was to be married.

★ ★ ★

It was a fairytale wedding with everyone in the settlement packing the church to see their hero marry the pretty girl, newly arrived from England. I was pleased to be invited, along with Major Fraser and the other officers of the garrison.

The bride was the sister of Edmund Maskelyne whose career in India had run parallel to that of Clive. He too, had been at Fort St George when it was captured by the French and had accompanied Clive on his daring escape. He had also enlisted in the military and was currently enduring a period of enforced idleness having been paroled by the French after being captured at Arcot.

Margaret Maskelyne was just seventeen, Clive's junior by ten years, small and slim, with big eyes and a tender mouth. She was completely besotted with Clive, which suited her matchmaking brother admirably. He had brought her out to India for the sole purpose of finding her a husband, and who better than his rich and most eligible friend.

Those who professed to know Clive better than I, said he enjoyed the freedom of bachelorhood far too much to ever settle down with just one woman, but to me the couple seemed to be very much in love, and ten days later I stood with them at the sea gate waiting to be ferried out to the ship. I knew Hatton was returning to England on the same vessel but he had boarded earlier with the baggage as it was customary for Company employees from the lower orders to be quartered with the ships crew in the foc's'le. They were often found work to do during the voyage. One person I didn't expect to be travelling with us was Tobias.

Clive explained. 'When this ship arrived it brought a letter telling him his mother is in very poor health. She's a widow and getting on in years. It seems the poor lady's losing her mind. Toby has a very lucrative position here, in a year or two he will be an extremely wealthy man but he's giving it all up to go home and care for her, that's the sort of fellow he is.'

There was a large, colourful crowd at the water's edge. All the principle burghers of the settlement were there, as was Major Fraser and his staff from the garrison. He had brought with him a guard of honour who were drawn up smartly on the landing stage. I looked for Dan Coggins and Archie Fowler and felt curiously let down when I didn't see them.

The major had just called to those assembled to give three cheers when there was a commotion from the rear. A group of muscular natives pushed their way through the throng, making way for the distinguished figure of Devraj Rawal who stepped forward waving a hand and shouting, 'Lieutenant Neville, *sahib*! Lieutenant Neville, *sahib*!'

I was extremely embarrassed when the princely Indian merchant fell to his knees in front of me.

'You gave me back something without price, Lieutenant *sahib*,' he said. 'I must give you something precious in return.'

He pressed a small wooden box into my hands and before I had a chance to say anything he and his entourage had melted into the crowd.

'Come on, look lively, old Neville!'

Clive was shouting from the flat-bottomed boat that was to ferry us out to the awaiting ship. I clambered aboard and we were pushed off to the sound of hurrahs from those on the shore. Once all the waving was done I settled down in the boat and opened the box. It contained a large, colourless pebble. I took it in my hand. It had almost a greasy feel to it and a strange surface sheen like nothing I had ever seen before.

'What have you got there then?' Tobias asked.

'I have no idea. Devraj Rawal gave it to me on the beach. It looks like a stone of some sort.'

He took it and held it up, above his eyelevel, turning it this way and that in the sunlight. He gave a low whistle. 'This, my dear chap,' he whispered, 'is an uncut diamond, and I have never seen one as big. It must be worth a King's ransom.'

I was terribly embarrassed. 'I can't accept it. We'll have to go back to shore.'

'You keep it and enjoy it, old Neville,' Clive said. 'I know these people. You'd insult the man terribly if you tried to give it back.'

Using just one long oar, the Indian boatman steered us skilfully towards the *Admiral Vernon*. Tobias handed the diamond to Clive who weighed it in his hand.

'It really is a whopper isn't it?' he said with a grin. He put it back in the box and snapped the lid shut. 'You know, you may have a problem disposing of a stone of that size — that is of course if that's what you want to do.'

I shrugged my shoulders. I had yet to come to terms with possessing such a valuable item let alone deciding what I was going to do with it.

Clive nudged his young Jewish friend. 'You've got some good contacts in the diamond trade haven't you, old Toby?'

Tobias nodded and smiled. 'I have relatives in Amsterdam,' he said.

★ ★ ★

My cabin on the *Admiral Vernon* was nothing more than a poky cubbyhole. There was barely room to turn around and it had a smell that led me to assume that its previous occupant had not been too particular about personal hygiene. But it was luxury compared to conditions on the *Indefatigable*. There, my quarters had been nothing more than a draughty hammock slung between the cannons on the gun deck.

To begin with I enjoyed the novelty of being on a ship with nothing else to do but attend meals and promenade on the deck, chatting to my fellow passengers. The quick-witted and intelligent Tobias was interesting company and Clive's Margaret possessed a keen sense of humour and was a joy to be with. Unfortunately, the same could not be said for her husband. As the voyage progressed, so he became more and more ill tempered.

'Damn it, Neville!' he exploded one

morning. 'This is my honeymoon for pity's sake! Being cooped up in a tiny cabin with single bunks is hardly conducive to romance. I should have known better than to book passage on a ship named after Old Grog.'

'Old Grog?'

'Admiral Vernon. That's what they called him, don't y'know. He started the practise of watering down the ship's rum.'

Our discomfort increased when food had to be rationed because supplies were running low. When we reached Cape Town, Clive had had enough. He arranged for the four of us, together with Hatton, who had volunteered to be Clive's servant, to be transferred to the *Pelham*, an altogether roomier and better-provisioned ship. In spite of this, the tedium of the journey was beginning to take its toll. Hardly had we left the little Dutch settlement when it became my turn to be the grouch of the party. As a seaman on *HMS Indefatigable* I had been too busy to think about the ship's progress but as a passenger on an Indiaman with nothing, but nothing, to do, the voyage was infuriatingly slow and intolerably dull.

We were standing at the ship's rail, idly watching Table Mountain slowly disappear into the shimmering heat haze when Tobias remarked that this little piece of Holland with its orderly streets and pleasant gardens reminded him of a sunlit Manchester, where more of his relatives lived. This idle comment sent my thoughts racing! What in God's name would I find when I did get back home? Josh Napper mourning the loss of his daughter? My mother still playing the part of an aged nymphet and my father sunk even deeper into the slough of alcoholism? And would my little brother still be in awe of the suave, charming and unbearably popular Edwin Cruikshank?

Tobias must have read my thoughts. 'Things invariably turn out to be not as bad as you imagine them to be,' he said gently.

I mentally shook myself out of my reverie. 'I'm sorry, it's just that I find the slowness of this voyage damned frustrating. Everything was in such a mess at home the last time I was there that I shudder to think what it's like now.'

'If there's anything I can do to help you only have to ask.'

I thought about his sick mother. 'You'll have your own things to attend to.'

My hand was on the rail. Tobias covered it with his. 'I mean what I say, Thomas,' he said.

★　★　★

The journey from Madras took seven months and although I had been away for almost two years I returned to an England that was not all that different to the one I had left. George II was still on the throne and the country was still talking about Bonnie Prince Charlie's frighteningly successful rebellion when his tartan army some five thousand strong had fought its way to within one hundred miles of the nation's capital.

London was where our little party was to part company. They all came to see me off. I didn't envy Tobias and the Clives for having grand houses there as, to me, a city was all right for short visits. I was too much of a countryman to suffer the stench and the crowded streets for any length of time.

I had thought long and hard about the gemstone and as I said goodbye to Tobias I handed it to him, still in the box as Devraj Rawal had given it to me.

'Could you get this to your relatives in Amsterdam and ask them to value it?'

'Of course,' he said with a smile and as I turned to speak to Clive and Margaret, he whispered, 'I am greatly honoured to have your trust, Thomas.'

Then, after much backslapping from my good friend and mentor and a few tears from his wife, I climbed aboard the coach.

'I fear I shall be monstrously bored in London, old Neville,' Clive shouted to me as we pulled out of the yard.

★ ★ ★

Before leaving Madras I had Clive's tailor
make me another scarlet coat, and dressed in
this, together with all the correct accoutre-
ments, I marched smartly up to the sentry on
duty outside the barracks and asked to see
the colonel. I was shown to his room where
my uncle leapt to his feet and grasped me
firmly by the hand.

'It's good to see you, my boy,' he bellowed.

He repeated this sentiment over and over
again whilst vigorously pumping my arm up
and down and slapping me on the shoulder. I
was greatly relieved when I was eventually
released.

'I sent a stiff note to their Lordships of the
Admiralty,' he said. 'How dare they press one
of my officers! I've not had a reply — and I'm
not surprised. Too damned ashamed of
themselves I shouldn't wonder.'

Colonel Reuben Neville, although younger
than my father and of a slightly heavier build
was, both in looks and voice, uncannily like
him. And, like my father, he was also honest
and fair, which made him a well-respected
and effective commanding officer.

He sat down and all signs of his happiness
at seeing me again seemed to drain from his
face, leaving it looking serious and grim.

'Now, I don't interfere in the running of the estate, as well you know, Thomas,' he said. 'It's not my concern and never has been. It passed on to your father along with the title . . . and quite right too! I've no quarrel with that. But, damn it, I'm a Neville too! He has no right to sell land that has been in the family for generations.'

'Father had to let go of some of the old church property to pay his debts. I knew about that before the Navy collared me.'

'Well it's been bought by a padre of sorts, did you know that? The fellow's rebuilt the old priory, stained glass windows, cloisters, the lot.' he grunted angrily. 'Still, I suppose it'll look all right from the Hall when it's weathered a bit.'

I steeled myself to ask the question I was longing to ask even though I was afraid of the answer.

'What of my parents?'

'They . . . er . . . when I got your letter from India I sent a galloper to let them know you were all right.'

'How *are* they?'

He stood up and paced the floor. 'Your father is a very sick man,' he said at length.

'And my mother?'

'I'm sorry to be the one to tell you this, Thomas, but I think your father's problems

151

have unbalanced her mind. She's all right physically and I'm sure she's happy enough, but she acts like a child . . . Take some leave. Take as long as you like. Go home lad, your parents need you.'

I touched my hat, did a smart about-turn and had a hand on the doorknob when he called out: 'And next time you report to me, young Neville, I want to see you properly dressed!'

I froze. What on earth could be wrong? I had taken a lot of trouble with my appearance. I was actually rather proud of how well I looked. Clive's tailor had made a splendid job of the coat and everything else I was wearing came from the military outfitters in Chester, where all the regiment's officers purchased their kit. I turned to face my commanding officer and stood to attention.

'Your pardon, sir,' I said. 'What is it about my appearance that offends you?'

He smiled. 'You've moved up in seniority while you've been away, my boy. You're wearing incorrect badges of rank, *Major* Neville.'

★ ★ ★

I left the Manchester stage at Knutsford where I hired a horse and set off across

152

country to Josh Napper's place. I had to find out about Emily.

To begin with it felt good to be trotting along the familiar lanes but I hadn't gone far before I sensed there was something wrong. I had always enjoyed swapping good-humoured banter with the workers in the fields but on this occasion as I rode past all I got in return were sullen looks, and one man even shook his fist. And where were the rosy-cheeked children that normally filled the village street with their shouting and their laughter? The odd ones I did catch a glimpse of looked old for their years, their little faces pinched and grey.

There was even a beggar at the gate to Napper's yard, and that was something I had never seen in Goostrey before. He was wrapped in a hooded cloak from which a bony arm protruded, a tin cup held in a skeletal hand.

'Spare a copper, Captain. I've quite forgot the last time I had a decent meal.'

A rumbling cough erupted from somewhere deep down in his chest and when it was over he was left gasping for breath. I took a guinea from my purse and dropped it into the cup.

'God bless you, Captain,' he wheezed, getting unsteadily to his feet.

As he stood up the hood slipped from his head. I recognised him instantly and I was angry. It was Nathan Craddock, the man my father had struggled to build the almshouses for.

'Craddock, it's me, Thomas Neville,' I said. 'Why in God's name are you begging in the street?'

He fished the coin out of the cup and threw it at my horse's feet. 'I can do without a Neville's charity,' he said. 'Your sort don't care about the likes of me.' He spat on the ground. 'When you gets too old to work and can't pay the rent then out you go! I'm in the street because that's where you Neville's put me!'

He stomped away, a silly, stubborn, cantankerous, proud old man.

★　★　★

There was something different about Napper's yard and it wasn't just the row of elegant carriages that were lined up in front of the stables, although to see so many here at one time was in itself unusual. A small bonfire smouldered in a corner, which I assumed had been lit to dispose of the loose hay and straw that normally littered the cobbles — and that was it! The place had been swept uncommonly clean, and come to think about it, there was a very un-Simon-like precision in the way those carriages had been lined up. Someone new must be looking after Josh's stables, I thought.

It wasn't long before I was to find out who that someone was, for beyond a smart *brougham* a man with a yard broom was busily sweeping. It was Sergeant Finch. It was such a surprise and a delight to see my old friend and tutor again. I quickly slid down from my horse and, shouting his name, I ran over to him. He turned and with a whoop of joy, he seized me in a fierce bear hug.

When he finally released me, he said, 'They told me you were in foreign parts, Master Thomas, India, wasn't it?'

I begged him for news of Emily.

He avoided my eyes and fumbled in his waistcoat pockets from where he eventually produced a stubby, brown, clay pipe. 'We didn't find her,' he said.

My throat constricted and tears burned my eyes. Somewhere deep down I had known all along that Emily wouldn't be here but that didn't make Finch's confirmation any easier to bear.

He opened a small leather bag and began stuffing tobacco into the pipe's tiny bowl. 'By the time we found the right dock, the slaver had sailed, bound for the Carolinas it was. I couldn't get Joshua to leave the quayside. He said he was going to sign on as a deckhand on the very next boat to the colonies, and no amount of talking on my part would make him change his mind. So I gave him what little money I had with me and wished him luck. I said I'd look after his tenancy 'til he came back.'

I felt in need of a drink, and something a little stronger than Josh's home brew. I asked who was looking after the tavern. Somehow I couldn't imagine grouchy old Simon playing the part of the genial host.

'Master Norbury, sir,' Finch said with a grin. 'He's taken to the job like a duck to water he has. But if you were thinking of going in the taproom, sir, I'd think again if I was you. The place is full of coachmen what belong to a rum lot that's up at the priory. It's good for business as we get to stable their horses and provide them with lodging for the weekend but they're no better than their masters.'

Gripping the small pipe in his teeth, he disturbed the edge of the bonfire with his foot. 'They've been drinking steady all morning and if a stranger was to put his nose through that door now like as not he'd be thrown out in the street without his breeches.'

156

I was tired after my long journey and I could well do without being pushed into teaching a group of drunks a lesson, so I remounted my horse.

'Where will I find Cruikshank?'

'He'll be at the priory, sir.'

Bending down, he selected a piece of smouldering wood from the fire, held it to the bowl of his pipe and sucked hard at the clay. Eventually a long tendril of smoke issued from between his lips and when he was satisfied that the tobacco was well lit he threw the brand back into the fire. After a few more noisy sucks he took the pipe from his mouth, spat on the ground and wiped his lips with the back of his hand.

'He lives there now, sir, since he had Master Ashley rebuild the old place.'

'Ashley rebuilt it?'

'Oh, yes, sir, and pleased to have the work he was, seeing as how them almshouses never got finished.'

The old cavalryman looked inquisitively at the pipe's smouldering contents before putting it back in his mouth. Then, with the short clay clenched firmly between his teeth, he said with a broad grin, 'You should see him now, sir. Talk about falling on your feet! There was a time when Master Ashley didn't have two pennies to rub together, now he comes here every day and Norbury cooks him luncheon, with no expense spared.'

I nodded my head in the direction of the carriages. 'Who *are* these people?'

His face lost its smile. He looked around the yard and lowered his voice. 'Master Cruikshank's friends, sir. Call themselves, the Bucks' Club. Sir Vivian's coachman tells me his master belongs to something like it in the south, only that goes under the name of the Hellfire Club down there he says. They're all wealthy young men from good families who, if you'll forgive me for saying so, sir, really should have better things to do with their time. They meets up at the priory for a long weekend once a month and there's right goings-on up there, I can tell you. Ben Sorrel, the poacher, says they dresses up in robes like monks wear and there's lots of chanting and incense swinging and the like, just like in church. And they brings women with them too, sir, and I don't mean ladies — if you gets my meaning.'

I turned my horse's head to leave.

'Just hold on a moment, sir,' he said, and gave a shrill whistle. There was a scrabbling noise from within the stable and a second later a dog came bounding out into the yard. She was a little heavier than the last time I saw her but it was Hagar all right. I reached down and let her nuzzle a wet nose into my hand, her rear end quivering with pleasure.

We set off along the narrow, sun-dappled lane past the church and towards the heath. On either side birds twittered unseen in the thick hawthorn hedges, and in some far-off field a calf was calling for its mother. It felt good to have a good horse between my knees and a dog scurrying to and fro at its feet.

Up on the bleak, windswept common where nothing will grow but gorse and brambles I stopped to take a deep breath, consciously filling my lungs with cool, fresh, English air. It all seemed a very long way from India, and when the many gables of Dunmere Hall came into sight, their sharp angles contrasting with the smooth, natural slopes of the distant Derbyshire peaks, it was as if I had never been away.

I was about to turn my horse onto the long drive up to the house when I saw a poor country girl gathering mushrooms. She was tall and thin with an apron of sacking draped around a foolishly impractical diaphanous garment, which had obviously once been a party frock, no doubt given to her by some kindly benefactor. At the sound of my horse's hooves she shot up like a startled rabbit looking ready to bolt. Her bonnet hid her face but there was something familiar about her that I could not quite put my finger on.

'Wait!' I called, spurring my horse into a trot to have a closer look.

'I wasn't doing any harm, sir,' she said, 'I was just gathering some mushrooms for breakfast.' She held out the pitiful little handful of fungi for my inspection. Her voice was cultured and one I recognised immediately although she showed no sign of recognising me, the lovely cornflower-blue eyes in her aristocratic if slightly dirty face remaining quite expressionless.

I slid from the saddle and grasped her by the shoulders. 'Don't you know me?' I gasped.

She wriggled from my grip but then Hagar ran up to her wagging her tail and for a long moment she stared first at the dog and then at me, a puzzled frown creasing her forehead.

'I own, sir,' she said. 'You do stir something in my memory.' Then she giggled coquettishly. 'Anyway, all you young men look alike in your robes and there are never any names at the priory are there, but then, that's the idea isn't it?' She lowered her eyes and in a breathless whisper, said, 'Perhaps you would like to remind me, sir?'

I backed away praying that when she got over this nonsense my mother wouldn't remember propositioning her own son.

'Not so bold on our own are we?' she cried, and with a merry laugh she slipped away into the undergrowth and was quickly lost to sight.

8

There was no sign of life at the Hall. I tied my horse to the iron ring set in the wall of the gatehouse and walked across the courtyard to the hall porch and hammered loudly on the door. It was opened by Mandrake, his gaunt face as emotionless as ever although I thought I caught a flicker of surprise in his eyes. He stood blocking the entrance.

'The Master is not here, sir,' he said coldly.

'Get someone to see to my horse will you, Mandrake,' I said. He didn't budge. 'And if you will kindly stand aside, I'll go to my room.'

'Owing to a deficiency of staff,' he intoned, 'many of the rooms in the house have been closed. I regret yours is one of them.'

Was this really happening? Was this man actually denying me entry into my own home?

'Let's not be silly about this,' I said. 'All my things are in that room.'

'Everything has been carefully packed in a large chest. If you let me know where you would like it to be sent I'm sure The Master will arrange it.'

I struggled to keep my temper in check. 'And the master is not here?'

'The Master, sir, lives at the priory.'

Whoa there! Finch said Edwin Cruikshank lives at the priory. Cruikshank brought this macabre servant here so I suppose it was only natural that he would think of him as 'The Master'?

'I meant Sir Rupert Neville,' I said.

'I do believe Sir Rupert is in the garden, sir.'

Well, at least that was some good news. If father was taking a turn in the garden he must be his old self again.

'Then kindly inform Master Giles I am here,' I said.

'Master Giles now resides at the Vicarage, sir,' the servant replied, 'but Master Ashley is here. I could enquire if he can see you?'

Ashley? What would he be doing here? Had my father's health and fortune improved to the point where he was once again involved in his 'good works'? Perhaps the almshouse project was underway once more.

Having said I would be pleased to see Master Ashley, I experienced the novelty of being shown to my father's study like a visitor to the house.

The difference in the architect's appearance was truly remarkable. The days of the frayed cuffs and the half-starved look were clearly long gone. He was dressed all in black as was the custom of men of his profession and although his tailor had done much to try to hide the fact, he had put on a lot of weight. His cheeks were quite chubby and a double chin rested heavily upon a crisp, white clerical collar. Master Ashley looked as though he had indeed 'fallen on his feet' as Sergeant Finch had so aptly put it.

He did not ask me to sit, but I did so all the same. Damn it! It *was* my father's study after all. After the formalities I asked about the almshouses.

'Oh, I do very little in that line nowadays,' he said with annoying superiority. 'My last building project was the old priory and since then I have been kept busy managing the estate.'

Managing the estate? No, it couldn't be! But yet here he was, sitting at my father's desk.

I took a deep breath and asked, 'And what estate would that be?'

He smiled a superior, looking-down-his-nose sort of smile. 'Why, *this* estate of course, Master Thomas, the Neville estate, although we *are* considering a change of name.

'It had been allowed to slip into a deplorable state,' he continued, looking at me accusingly. 'Did you know, for instance, that rents have not been increased for years, and unprofitable tenants have been allowed to remain on their farms?

'Well, I've put a stop to all that mollycoddling nonsense! A tenant either pays the landowner his due or out he goes, bag and baggage!'

I leapt to my feet. 'And be replaced with whom?' I demanded. 'Of course, with your long experience of land management you will know dozens of experienced farmers anxious to take on unprofitable tenancies?' It was unlike me to be sarcastic but the man was annoying me.

'We've done all right thus far,' he mumbled and sat without speaking for a moment, and then he looked me straight in the eye and said, 'Anyway, I have plans to rip out a lot of the old hedges and give my loyal tenants bigger farms to run.'

'And change the appearance of the countryside?'

'Already done that,' he said with a sneer. 'Remember that area of woodland over on the Derbyshire border? I had it all cut down for timber.'

I gasped. 'But some of those trees were hundreds of years old! That was once part of the Great Macclesfield Forest where the

English kings would come to hunt wild boar.'

Ashley shuffled the papers on the desk. 'That is precisely what's wrong with your family,' he said. 'You are too sentimental by half. I view things in a more practical light. I have contacts in shipbuilding you see, and I know they can't get enough of those old twisted oaks. Shipwrights love them because they make powerful brackets that will hold a vessel together in the heaviest seas.' He sat back with a smug look. 'And not only did the estate profit from the sale of the trees, we gained thereabouts of forty acres of land that we can cultivate and make even more money from.'

The job of estate manager had obviously given full rein to the heartless, money-grubbing side of Jacob Ashley's character and it was all I could do not to haul him across my father's desk and slap his supercilious, well-fed face.

My father! It was he I had come to see and not to waste time with this detestable person. I stormed out of the study and behind me, I heard Ashley shouting for Mandrake. The tall servant and I met in the great hall. I'd had enough of being treated like a stranger in my own home so I grabbed him by the lapels of his coat and demanded to be told precisely where my father was at that very moment.

'You will find Sir Rupert in the Orangery, sir,' he croaked.

The Orangery was a large, curved, south facing stone conservatory with tall, gothic windows. It had been built with the object of encouraging tender, exotic plants that would otherwise fail in the extremes of the English climate to grow and flourish in its warm sunlit interior. As a boy I was forbidden to play there, not that I ever particularly wanted to as its moss-covered, stone-flagged floor was always slimy and wet and the whole building smelled of decaying vegetation. But my father loved the place.

He was seated in a cane chair with a rug across his knees. I was pleased to note that there was some colour in his cheeks and the dark circles had gone from his eyes but I quickly realised that I was looking at my father and what I was seeing was an old man with all the vigour and energy drained out of him. He didn't look round as I came in but just sat staring out of the window. There was an empty glass on a small table by his side. I picked it up and sniffed. It had held brandy, a good cognac by the smell. I could hear him now. 'Brandy should be allowed to age slowly in cool, damp cellars, Thomas, to soften the spirit and develop the bouquet'.

In retrospect it seems rather inadequate but

all I could think of to say was, 'Hello, Father.'

'Any problems with the tenants, Thomas?' he asked. 'It's good for someone from the family to get out and see how they are managing their properties. Being a landowner is a sacred trust, my boy.'

I had never thought of my father in terms of love. My feelings for him had always been more of respect and admiration. I envied his clarity of thought and the strength of his resolve. I admired his honesty and applauded his philanthropy but he had always distanced himself from me. I dearly wanted to touch him, hold his hand, do something, but I couldn't, it wouldn't be right.

'Nathan Craddock's wife dying on him like that last winter seems to have knocked the stuffing right out of the poor fellow,' he said. 'We must get on with those almshouses so that folk like him can be properly cared for.' He lifted his empty glass and peered at it. 'Ask Norbury to fetch me another brandy will you? Or, on second thoughts, I might try a little genever this time.'

'I'm sorry I've been away so long, Father,' I said and I walked away. He seemed happy enough living in the past, so I left him to it. I mounted my horse, whistled up Hagar and with a heavy heart rode back to Napper's tavern.

The carriages had gone from the yard and this time it was old Simon who came to take my horse. It was hard to judge his feelings for the Nevilles because he grumbled all the time anyway.

A most pleasant surprise awaited me in the taproom. Norbury was bending down with his back to the door filling a jug from one of the big wooden casks and who should be standing talking to him but my little brother. The slamming of the door caused them both to look round.

Giles bounded over to greet me, a big wide grin across his face. After hugging almost all the breath out of my body, he said, 'I see you're still a soldier then, Tom. What happened to the navy? I thought you'd be an Admiral by now.'

'The least said about my time before the mast the better. But what about you, I hear you're living at the Vicarage?'

He pulled a face. 'Yes, and Master Hulse's housekeeper is possibly the worst cook in the county. But you know her, Tom; she's a formidable woman. I've yet to meet a person brave enough to tell her so.' He steered me over to a table. 'Norbury! A tankard of ale for Master Thomas, and you can top mine up again while you're at it.'

'It is good to see you again, sir,' Norbury

said, his voice choked with emotion. He turned away quickly and I think I saw him wipe his eyes with the hem of his apron before returning to finish filling his jug.

Giles didn't seem any the worse for eating the vicar's housekeeper's food. He looked to be in the peak of condition and positively glowing with health, although perhaps slightly intoxicated.

'I am so glad you're here, Tom,' he said, still grinning from ear to ear. 'I'm being ordained soon, here at St Luke's, and I could do with having you with me for a bit of moral support.' He held out a trembling hand and we both laughed. 'Mamma will be there of course,' he said. 'Most of the time she's away with the fairies but my ordination is still very important to her.' Then suddenly becoming serious he said, 'Sergeant Finch said you'd been up to the hall.' I nodded. 'So you've seen for yourself what a state our father is in?'

Just at that moment Norbury banged two foaming tankards on the table. I realised then how thirsty I was and I drank so deeply from the mug that I almost emptied it. I then told Giles about the reception I'd received locally. His reaction was so uncharacteristically violent it took me by surprise.

'And who have we got to thank for that?' he shouted. 'I'll tell you who. Our beloved father, that's who.'

'Steady on, Giles. Everything was fine until he started gambling, and it was Edwin Cruikshank who set him on that road.'

'We should put our hands together and thank God for Edwin Cruikshank.'

At first I thought that this was perhaps another of my little brother's jokes but when it was obvious he wasn't going to suddenly burst out laughing, I said, 'Oh, come on! Edwin Cruikshank's nothing more than a smooth talking bastard who has brought our family nothing but grief.'

Giles took a long pull at his tankard before replying. 'The Reverend Cruikshank is my kind of priest, Tom. He's not one who's always telling you not to do this and not to do that! He says there's only one law and that is 'do what you will'.'

'I'm surprised you are bothering to get ordained,' I said cynically.

Giles put his tankard down and looked at me thoughtfully. 'It's funny you should say that, Tom,' he said. 'You know me. I only got involved in all this God-bothering stuff because Mamma insisted on it. Oh, I can put on a long face and do all that mumbo-jumbo like the rest of them. It's just a case of learning the patter, rather like being an actor really, and it's money for old rope — only I don't get any money, being non-stipendiary you understand — unlike the vicar, who gets what the Church laughingly calls a 'living'. No, it all depends on how my performance is received by my audience as to how much I get in the jolly old collection plate.' He pushed his tankard towards Norbury and raised his eyebrows as a signal that he wanted another. 'If it was up to me I'd chuck it all up tomorrow but Edwin seems keen on me going through with the ordination — and why shouldn't I? I deserve it after serving my time with Master Hulse.'

The door opened and Simon popped his head in. 'Your carriage awaits, Your Reverence,' he intoned with a knowing wink at Norbury.

'Oh, right,' Giles said. He seemed to be flustered. 'Must go, Tom, urgent business and all that. Tell you what; I'll join you for supper tonight. I can't wait to hear all about your adventures. The food here has improved tremendously now that old Norbury's in charge.'

And with that he was gone.

I looked at our former butler enquiringly. 'Carriage?' I asked.

Norbury smiled. 'The farm's market wagon, sir. Master Giles borrows it on occasion.'

'I would have thought a gig with a lively trotter would be more to my brother's taste.' I said. 'Why would he want a cumbersome old farm cart?'

It was Simon who had come back to the taproom without me noticing him who answered my question. 'On account of it being covered, Master Thomas,' he said. 'His Reverence uses it so's no one should know who he's got with him. But you ask Ben Sorrel who she is; he's seen the cart outside her cottage.'

'So my brother has a lady friend. What's so unusual about that?'

Old Simon stuck his bristly chin close to my ear, exuding a noxious odour of old ale and stale tobacco as he whispered, 'On account of him being a clergyman and her being a witch.'

For a moment I was speechless. The old ostler, clearly enjoying the look of incredulity that must be registering on my face, pressed on with relish, 'May the Good Lord forgive him,' he said, 'for it's Welsh Meg he's carrying on with, and he's having his fun with her in the back of our cart. Leastways, that's what Ben reckons.'

Now I was angry! How dare this garrulous old man who had always been well treated by my family actually revel in that rascally poacher's slanderous gossip about my brother!

173

'Yes, and we all know about Ben Sorrel's colourful stories don't we?' I snapped, hoping that the tenor of my reply and a stern look would scotch any further speculation and rumour.

I vowed to have strong words to say to that scoundrel Sorrel when next I saw him and as for my little brother, well, I could hardly wait until suppertime.

★ ★ ★

I spent the afternoon visiting some of the nearby farms, and from the way I was received it was obvious that the Nevilles were not the most popular family in the county. My father was viewed generally as a drunken rake and my mother a gratuitous wanton.

That evening I sat in the tavern's small dining room with a tankard of porter, reviewing the events of the day. I concluded that this had been possibly the most depressing day of my life. I desperately wanted to do something to help find Emily but somehow I had to wrest control of the Neville estate away from that smooth talking bastard, Edwin Cruikshank, and his avaricious lieutenant, Jacob Ashley. Legal action was out of the question. I couldn't bear to think of having to prove my parents culpably irresponsible or worse still, that they were insane.

And to add to it all, my brother was late for supper.

When he did eventually come bustling into the small dining room he seemed to be in high spirits.

'Why so glum, Tom,' he asked.

'Our family's reputation as benevolent landowners has been damned to hell by cold-blooded rent increases and heartless evictions, that's why!' I replied angrily and went on to tell him about my visit to the local tenants.

'Well, we'd sold all the family silver, old boy. There wasn't anything else left to do.' He gave me a brotherly slap on the back and sat down at the table. 'Listen, Norbury's got roast forequarter of lamb on tonight,' he said with a grin. 'I've had it here before. He does it well.'

'I don't know that I feel like eating,' I said morosely.

'Go on! You'll enjoy it. Just imagine it, young meat butchered no more than two or three days ago, then carefully roasted on a brisk, clean fire and basted continuously until it's ready for serving. It's delicious!'

I could keep it to myself no longer. 'What's this I hear about you and Megan Griffith?'

That took him by surprise. 'Who told you?' he asked.

'Never mind that! Is it true?'

Giles shrugged his shoulders. 'In a way,' he said, 'Oh, for goodness sake, Tom, what am I but a dull and boring, black-suited clergyman? Not the sort of image to set young girl's heart a'racing is it? And, not only am I a clergyman, but thanks to my father I'm a poor one at that! So you can perhaps understand why I am not exactly fighting off female company. You said yourself we are not the most popular family in the county, but Megan has never given a toss what people think . . . And I find her knowledge of natural remedies fascinating. Did you know, for example, that comfrey heals severed flesh, nettles can cure paralysis and marigold leaves are a treatment for smallpox?'

I shook my head and his eyes glinted. I knew him well enough to know he was about to disclose something he regarded as being top secret. He looked about him to see if he could be overheard.

'Monk's-hood and Belladonna in a drop of alcohol, Thomas, and you'll fly like a bird,' he whispered and waited for this snippet of information to sink in before continuing cheerfully with, 'And Hemlock's the thing if there's someone you want to be rid of. It induces paralysis that starts in the feet and moves slowly up the body. There's no pain or convulsions and the victim is able to think clearly until he dies, ultimately by asphyxia. Neat eh? Not that I've tried either, mind you,' he said grinning broadly.

'For goodness sake, Giles. Megan Griffith must be all of twenty years your senior!'

He grinned. 'But a handsome woman, Tom, you've got to grant me that,' he said, 'And I'm not thinking of marrying her,' he added with a wink.

I could see I was getting nowhere with this subject so I let it drop and over dinner our conversation drifted to the many happy times we had spent together as boys on the estate and more than once I was moved to discover that some trivial little incident that I had almost forgotten had remained an important event in my little brother's memory.

Norbury's roast lamb was every bit as good as Giles said it would be and as I passed my plate over for a second helping, a plan began to form in my mind. I now knew how I was going to regain control of the Neville estate and I knew who I needed to help me do it.

9

The nag that brought me from Knutsford had long since been returned so I went along to inspect old Simon's stock. I was very impressed with a handsome black stallion.

'He's a mite young, sir, and still a bit skittish,' he warned.

I ran a hand over his flank feeling the well-developed muscles quiver under my touch.

'Saddle him up, I'll take him,' I said.

As I placed my foot in the stirrup the fine beast turned its head, showing the whites of his eyes and when I was in the saddle he snorted and pawed the ground. I gave him his head and we were off through the night like the wind. Outside Frodsham I overtook a stagecoach and the guard, thinking I was a highwayman, reached for his blunderbuss although we were well out of range before he had time to cock the weapon. I gave him a cheery wave, and because I was so exhilarated by the ride, a loud halloo for good measure. I got to Chester barracks just as dawn was breaking.

The day starts early in the army and my

uncle was where I expected him to be, having breakfast. As usual he was the first down, so, apart from the mess staff, he was quite alone.

'Thomas, my dear boy,' he called across the empty dining room. 'Come, sit yourself down and have something to eat. This ham is very good.' He waved to one of the waiters who were hovering at the extremities of the room. 'Bring Major Neville some breakfast,' he shouted. 'Slice him some of that ham.'

A plate of meat appeared in front of me as if by magic. I cut off a small portion and tasted it. It was moist, sweet, lightly smoked, and just to my taste. I made a mental note to congratulate the commissary and took a larger piece.

Very slowly the room began to fill and I got the impression that had I not been there, my uncle would have thought about leaving, so that his officers could enjoy their meal without having to be on their best behaviour because their colonel was present. But for my sake he stayed where he was.

'How did you find things on the estate?' he asked.

'Very much as you described them, sir, which is why I'm here.'

The tables around us were filling up. I leaned forward and lowered my voice, 'I have a stratagem to take over control but I can only do it with your help.'

'I'm listening,' he said, his eyes twinkling.

'Mother asked that rascal, Cruikshank, to run things when my father's drinking got out of hand.'

'Yes, yes, I know that.'

'I suppose the kindest thing one can say about her now is that she is not herself at the moment so it's no good looking for help in that quarter.'

The colonel sighed. 'You're right there, lad. It's a tragedy, that's what it is.' A faraway look came into his eyes. 'We were both in love with her, you know, your father and me, but she married the better man, God damn it!' He struck the table with his fist, bringing the general buzz of conversation in the dining room to an abrupt end. 'What sort of life would she have had as a soldier's wife, moving from place to place all the time?' He realised that those present were looking at him expectantly. 'Carry on, gentlemen, carry on,' he said loudly, and then, in a stage whisper, meant only for me, 'What is this damn scheme of yours, Thomas? Come on, out with it, man!'

'The only way to wrest control of the estate away from Cruikshank, is for my father to order Jacob Ashley to go,' I said, and told him my plan.

'Capital! Capital! When do we start?'

'Very soon I hope, sir, but first I must get some money to pay off my father's debts.'

He looked genuinely concerned. 'You're very welcome to what little I've got but from what I hear you'll need a great deal to get your father out of trouble.'

'What I need, sir, is a pen, some writing paper and the services of a dispatch rider to take an urgent letter to London.'

He stood up and there was much scraping of chair legs as the others began to get to their feet.

'Carry on, gentlemen, carry on,' he said beaming amiably at the assembly. 'Come, Thomas. There's pens and paper in my office. You write your letter. I'll see you get the best galloper in the regiment to deliver it for you.'

* * *

I wrote to Robert Clive describing in some detail the present situation at Dunmere with specific reference to Edwin Cruikshank's evil influence over my family. I then penned a message to Tobias asking him to obtain what he could on Devraj Rawal's diamond, explaining that I needed money urgently and, if it would aid a quick sale, he had my permission to arrange to have the stone cut up. I also begged him to get the proceeds to me with all possible speed. I folded this letter and placed it inside the other, writing the address of Clive's London house in Queen Square clearly on the front and sealing the back with a blob of molten wax, into which I pressed my signet ring.

My uncle stood with me watching the courier ride off. 'Your letter will be delivered quickly, Thomas, never fear,' he said. 'Swift Nick Cartwright the lads call him. Some say Corporal Cartwright could outrun Dick Turpin himself.'

I'd heard that the story of this notorious highwayman's ride to York was itself stolen property and that it was one, John Nevison, who, in sixteen seventy-six, rode to that city in an unbelievably fast time, thereby establishing an alibi for a crime he had committed in Kent. But I kept this item of trivia to myself commenting only on the fine horse the corporal was riding.

'Aye, we may be a regiment of foot but we keep an excellent stable, and we know how to look after good horseflesh. Cartwright will stage his mounts at other military garrisons en route to the capital . . . and don't worry, he'll not be delayed by some bureaucratic sergeant-of-horse while he carries my warrant.'

If the Colonel of a regiment were to be killed or seriously wounded on the field of battle his senior major would step in and take over command immediately. But we were not at war so it took my uncle and his full headquarters staff the best part of two days to make arrangements for him to take a short leave of absence.

I thought we would draw less attention to ourselves if we were to travel in civilian clothes so when the day finally came that we were able to leave I dressed in an old but comfortable leather coat and some heavy tweed breeches that I had found still hanging in the wardrobe in my quarters. Unlike my rooms at Dunmere, these were just as I had left them, having being carefully attended to in my absence by Lance Corporal Barney Nolan, my batman, and one of the few Irishmen in the twenty-second. Although he would never acknowledge the fact, I had actually seen Nolan wipe a tear from his powder-blackened cheek the day I returned to the regiment.

My uncle said to meet him at the stables and I arrived to find him already there. A cold shiver ran down my spine for it could have been my father standing there. With him were our personal servants, or batmen, as they are called in the army because they are in charge of the bat horses that carry an officer's baggage. They also wore plain clothes, that is if you could call Lance Corporal Nolan's green jacket, and red and white spotted neckerchief, plain.

Our small party made only one stop, for lunch at the inn at Stamford Bridge. From there it was but a few hours to Goostrey.

As our small party neared the little timber-framed church dedicated to St Luke the Evangelist my eye was drawn to the mighty yew that stands before its entrance. Some say this evergreen tree is planted in village churchyards because it represents everlasting life, but like countless others, this monster was planted for purely utilitarian reasons. Yew provided the best wood for making the English longbow but its leaves are poisonous to pigs and cattle. The only place in a village sure to be fenced off from livestock was the churchyard.

'Not far now, eh?'

My uncle's voice brought me out of my daydream. I was now level with the ancient tree, which, with changing times, had now become a convenient place to tether a horse. The horse on this occasion was between the shafts of a cart that I recognised as belonging to Napper's Farm.

'I want to make a brief stop here if you don't mind,' I called back.

Leaving the batmen to look after our horses I took my uncle into the church.

It was just as gloomy as I remembered it; the only light was that filtering in through the stained glass windows. It had a dank, unlived-in smell and a silence that forced you to speak in a reverent whisper. It was also as cold as a tomb.

I heard a noise, a muffled sound of voices coming from the vestry. And laughter, yes, there it was again, a woman laughing. Bidding my uncle to wait where he was, I went to the vestry door and pushed it open. The antiquated hinges creaked, and within the tiny room there was frantic activity. I caught a glimpse of naked thighs and loose-fitting garments being hurriedly shaken down to their full length.

Giles turned aggressively to meet the intruder head on. His face collapsed into a silly grin when he saw who it was.

'Phew! It's only you, Tom. For a terrible moment there I thought it was the Rural Dean . . . Got to keep the old slate clean until the big day, what?' He giggled self-consciously. 'You know Megan?' he said.

The woman turned. Our eyes met and I

caught my breath. I had never been this close to the wicked lady of the village before. Her face was nut-brown like a gypsy's, heart-shaped with a pointed chin. She had high cheekbones, large, brown, hypnotic eyes and the most fascinatingly attractive mouth I had ever seen. It was small with unusually deep laughter lines bracketing its corners and a top lip that projected ever so slightly over the bottom one. The whole effect was that she was both pouting and laughing at you at the same time.

Good manners dictated that I should bow, but a reluctance to tear my eyes away from her reduced the movement to little more than a sharp nod of my head.

'I am acquainted with your brother, madam,' I said, congratulating myself on my diplomacy. She raised an inquisitive eyebrow, so I added quickly, 'The Reverend Cruikshank.'

'So, *you* are Tom,' she whispered slowly in a low, husky voice. 'The soldier-boy.' Then, with a toss of her long black hair, she laughed, and I was utterly captivated.

'I fear you have misunderstood the Reverend Cruikshank. To him we are all brothers and sisters . . . Is it not the same with your Master Hulse?'

'Soldier-boy'. I quite liked that. It made me

smile. Her voice was seductive and her eyes were flirtatious. I am ashamed to say she aroused feelings within me that had lain dormant for far too long.

At that moment my uncle's face appeared at the door. 'Are you going to be much longer, Thomas?' he demanded. 'Only it's damned cold out here.'

Suddenly realizing where he was and assuming the cleric in the dingy little room was the Reverend Hulse, he mumbled an embarrassed, 'Sorry, Vicar,' and ducked out again.

'The vicar's not here,' Giles called out. 'There's just me and, and one of my parishioners. We were, er, having a fellowship meeting.'

I was grateful that the young rascal managed to stifle a giggle for had he begun to laugh I would have been unable to prevent myself from joining in.

'Good Lord!' Giles said. 'Was that Father? How on earth did you manage to get the old boy sobered up?'

I didn't answer his question. My spur-of-the-moment experiment had been a resounding success, and because Megan's evocative glances were making me feel decidedly uncomfortable I bid them both 'good day' and beat a hasty retreat.

* * *

It was dusk by the time our party rode into the cobbled courtyard at Napper's Farm. Finch came out to meet us and, just as Giles had done, he also took Uncle Reuben to be Sir Rupert. This boosted my confidence in the scheme I had planned for the following day.

In the well-lit taproom it was a different story. Norbury didn't look twice at my uncle, and went on quietly with his work.

'Don't you think he looks like my father?' I asked him when I went over for some drinks.

'The two brothers were always very much alike, sir,' he said. 'I have not seen Colonel Neville since the day your father married your mother . . . He is as I imagined he would be after all those years.'

I was beginning to worry about tomorrow. 'But he could pass as my father, do you think?'

Norbury was not enjoying this. 'Colonel Neville is a younger man, sir, and very fit,' he said, and seeing I was not to be put off with only half an answer, he cleared his throat and added, 'A gentleman's appearance is markedly affected by circumstance, sir. Colonel Neville's voice and mannerisms are so like your father's that to me he is as Sir Rupert was but a few years ago, before all these recent trials and tribulations took their toll. No, sir, I regret to say that now there is no mistaking Colonel Neville for your father — unless, of course, the gentleman had the light behind him.'

But of course! With Giles it was the gloom of the church and Finch the dusk of evening. My little ruse could still work if I stage-managed it properly.

★ ★ ★

Clouds rolled in overnight and the following day dawned grey and overcast. There was an unseasonable cold wind from the north that brought with it wintry showers that were quite heavy at times. I feared that Jacob Ashley would not show up on such a day and I said as much to Norbury as we were preparing the stage for my little drama.

'He'll be here, sir. I promised him roast pork today — and that's his favourite.' The old butler laughed. 'Master Ashley would ride through floodwater if needs be for my crispy roast pork.'

Norbury's confidence went some way to reassure me but there was still something odd about the whole business.

'Why does he come here for lunch every

day?' I asked. 'Does he not get fed at home?'

'Mistress Ashley is a strong minded woman, sir. She has raised nine children, and is a firm believer in simple food, oat porridge for breakfast, bread and cheese for lunch — perhaps some soup on a cold day — and a good hot meal of meat and vegetables for supper — fish, of course, on Fridays. Furthermore, sir, she does not approve of strong drink so all meals are accompanied only by water, or 'Adam's ale' as she calls it.' He leaned forward and lowered his voice. 'I'm given to understand, sir, that she is also something of a scold.'

Ashley's favourite table was the one immediately in front of the fireplace but with the wind roaring in the chimney I had the perfect opportunity to have him placed by a window, with his back to it. The plan was for Uncle Reuben and I to hide by the kitchen door behind the stairs until Ashley was busy eating his meal. I would then enter and engage him in conversation, allowing my uncle to slip in unseen and take up a position on the window seat behind him. We had a quick rehearsal with me playing the part of Ashley. It was just as Norbury said; with the light behind him, my uncle could well be my father.

Uncle Rupert and I stood waiting beneath

the stairs for what seemed an interminable age. The one redeeming feature of our hidey-hole was that the smell of roast pork from the kitchen was infinitely preferable to the combination of wood smoke, tobacco and stale beer in the taproom. Each time the door opened we tensed. The first to arrive were some villagers, and then a couple of drovers burst in to escape from the rain, but Norbury played his part well and steered them all well away from our little stage.

Finally our quarry arrived, in a black, caped riding coat that made him look like a great fat beetle. He took off his hat and shook the water from it onto the sawdust-strewn floor.

'Ho there! Innkeeper!' he shouted.

Norbury was quick off the mark to take the estate manager's wet coat and hat. I hoped he wasn't being noticeably over attentive. I caught my breath when Ashley queried the change of table but Norbury didn't bat an eyelid.

'A north wind has a tendency to blow smoke into the room, sir, so I took the liberty of setting you a place away from the fireplace.' He drew out the chair at the table by the window. 'You can still enjoy a view of the fire from here, sir, and have the benefit of what little warmth there is in the sun today on your back.'

'Very well then,' Ashley said, resignedly. He sat down, and I breathed a sigh of relief.

Well done Norbury, I breathed. You couldn't have handled that scene better if we'd rehearsed it a dozen times.

Ashley was well into his plate of roast pork when I made my move. He called for more wine and I took it to him. Without looking up from his plate, he asked for more crackling.

'I think you are quite fat enough, Master Ashley,' I replied, sitting down opposite him. In his surprise he must have swallowed a piece of meat whole as he suddenly collapsed in a fit of coughing. I felt like cheering as my uncle took this golden opportunity to move across to the window recess. I made sure Ashley's attention was well and truly diverted by handing him his glass of wine, which he snatched from me and gulped down greedily.

'I was on my way to see you, Master Ashley,' I lied. 'Now I am home again my father would like me to take over the running of the estate.'

'Cruikshank put *me* in charge!' he spluttered.

From the window seat my uncle said, 'The Neville estate belongs to me, sir, not Master Cruikshank.'

Ashley spun round, his chin still wet with wine.

'And it is my wish,' Uncle Reuben continued, 'That my son and heir should manage it. He will take up this responsibility with immediate effect. You may return to the Hall and collect any belongings you may have there, but after today I do not wish to see you in my study again unless you are sent for. Is that understood?'

It was a masterly performance. For a moment even I thought I was listening to my father. Ashley blushed a deep crimson.

'Yes, yes, of course Sir Rupert,' he stammered, scrabbling out of his chair.

Norbury appeared as if by magic with his coat and hat. Ashley snatched them from him and fled from the taproom, his napkin still tied around his fat neck.

We looked at each other, Uncle Reuben, Norbury and I, and suddenly we all burst out laughing. The tension was over. The plan had worked.

'Well done all round,' my uncle said, wiping the tears from his eyes. 'It's good to know the estate is back in the family's hands again.'

Finch had instructions to delay Ashley for as long as he dared, and old Simon was waiting out of sight in the barn with a horse saddled up for me. My plan was to gallop to the hall and get my father safely out of the way before Ashley arrived there and saw him. I would then use the grasping former architect to confirm I was now managing the estate, and rid it of all Cruikshank's appointees, starting with his sinister butler, Mandrake.

I pulled on my coat and was about to leave for the barn when Corporal Prescott, my uncle's batman, came bursting into the room and almost collided with me.

'There's a coach just pulled in, sir, and the gentleman is asking for you,' he said excitedly.

The colonel stepped out of the window recess. 'That's no way to make a report, corporal!' he snapped. 'What's the damned fellow's name?'

The batman snapped to attention. 'I have the honour to report, sir, that a gentleman by the name of Bloom is asking for the Major, sir!'

Tobias! By all that's wonderful, this *was* good news. 'Where is this gentleman, Corporal?' I asked.

'I have the honour to report, sir . . . '

'Yes, yes. Get on with it, man,' my uncle growled.

'The gentleman has gone to relieve himself, sir. I sent the coach up to the stables.'

As much as I wanted to see my friend and companion from the long voyage home, getting to the hall before Ashley was vital to the success of the plan.

'A right splendid coach it is too,' the corporal was saying to Norbury. 'A big four-in-hand with two flunkeys up, as well as a driver. This Tobias Bloom must be a very important man.'

I saw my uncle looking daggers at his talkative batman so I quickly shooed Prescott out of the door, suggesting he show the newly arrived servants to the kitchen for some refreshment and then give Finch a hand with the horses.

Minutes passed and Tobias still hadn't put in an appearance. I felt I was cutting things a little too fine.

'I'm sorry uncle, but I really have to go,' I said. 'Finch won't be able to delay Ashley indefinitely and if he gets back to the hall before me and sees my father then all the good work we have done today will be for nothing. Please apologise to Master Bloom for me. He's a good friend, you can tell him everything.'

Suddenly I had the most wonderful idea.

'Tell him he's to come to the hall for dinner tonight. You'll come too won't you, sir? You can ride over together.'

His face clouded. 'Er, I won't if you don't mind, Thomas,' he said. 'On the day your mother and father wed, I vowed I'd never set foot in Dunmere Hall again.'

He stared straight ahead as he spoke, his chin jutting forward defiantly.

'That may sound a bit melodramatic. I couldn't bear the thought of seeing her happily married to someone else, y'see.'

I didn't have time to mince my words.

'Mother won't be there. She lives at the priory with Edwin Cruikshank.'

He went suddenly very quiet and I sensed that my remark had hurt him. I could see all manner of questions trembling on his lips but when he spoke again, all he said was, 'In that case I'll be pleased to come.'

I had expected Simon to be at the barn but Nolan was also there, mounted and waiting. The old ostler held the stirrup for my foot and I swung up into the saddle.

'Simon, ask Norbury to tell everyone who used to work below stairs at the hall that I plan to have a dinner party there tonight . . . and send word to my little brother. Tell him he's invited.'

10

Later that afternoon, Mandrake led a sorry little procession away from the hall, the overweight architect bringing up the rear. It was quite comical to watch Jacob Ashley struggling to carry a large portmanteau whilst Hagar ran around him, snapping at his heels.

I allowed myself a brief smile of satisfaction. 'Out you go, Master Ashley,' I whispered. 'Bag and baggage.'

The splendid animal that Ashley had ridden to Napper's Farm was back in the Neville stables where it belonged.

And in that same stable block, concealed in the comfortable quarters formerly occupied by Sergeant Finch, was my father. I intended bringing him back to the house once Cruikshank's people were out of the way, and before he drank too much from that bottle of cognac he'd insisted on taking with him when I installed him there.

* * *

Norbury was the first of the former servants to arrive. I'd gone to the kitchen to see just

197

how many retainers we had left and found old Polly, the scullery maid, and her half-witted daughter, Nancy, standing with their backs to the row of sinks, wringing their aprons nervously. A polite cough from the other side of the door caused me to look behind it.

'My God, Norbury, where did you spring from?' I gasped.

The old butler maintained a dignified reserve but there was a twinkle in his eye when he said, 'I'm sorry if I startled you, sir, but there are ways into this old place that even you don't know.' He fixed the two dishwashers with a stern look. 'I was endeavouring to ascertain if this is the extent of my staff.'

'There's a young groom up at the stables, but all I've found in the house, apart from these two, is the boot boy.'

'Sergeant Finch is out in the farm cart at this very moment, sir,' Norbury said. 'I've asked him to collect three chambermaids and two footmen — their families all live in the village — and Cook, who is staying with her sister at Allostock . . . ' He did his butler's polite cough. 'Er, about your valet, sir?' he ventured.

'Lance Corporal Nolan? My batman?'

'Precisely, sir, a fine fellow. I saw him earlier in the yard. I'm sure he would welcome something to do. Might I suggest we ask him to make up the beds — and check on the fires, he can have the boot boy to help him. Polly and her daughter can make a start on the vegetables while I see what meat we have, there should at least be a ham, or some game.'

It suddenly occurred to me that I had selfishly robbed Josh's place of its resident chef and master of the house.

'Will Finch go back to Napper's Farm after he has delivered your staff?' I asked.

'Oh, no, sir. He says he feels it is duty to stay on here and look after your guest's horses, but if you were to ask me, sir, I would say he can't wait to take a broom to the stables. He's been fretting about them all the time he's been at Napper's Farm.'

'But who's to run the tavern?'

'The coach Master Bloom arrived in, sir, belongs to a Robert Clive, as do the servants that came with it. I'm told the coachman also controls his master's household in London, although as far as I know he hasn't any domestic service experience. Sergeant Finch took to him as soon as they met. Then he would, sir, wouldn't he, them having both been timeserving soldiers in the army.' he gave a disapproving sniff.

Now I understood why the coach was so

grand. 'Would this coachman's name be Hatton by any chance?'

Norbury looked surprised. 'Indeed it is, sir. Do you know the man?'

'Yes I do!' I said delightedly. 'And have no fear about the tavern, Norbury. Company Sergeant Major Hatton is a *very* capable man.'

I returned my father to his favourite chair in the Orangery and, turning a deaf ear to his repeated requests for more brandy, I settled him down with a book from the library and a cup of chicken broth, a pan of which I had found simmering on the kitchen range.

On my way back to the house I encountered the wagon from Napper's Farm, disgorging its passengers under the watchful eye of Sergeant Finch. I saw the old soldier help Cook down. It was obvious to me that this was to prevent the amply proportioned woman from tipping the cart over, but to her it was a gallant gesture and she simpered like a young girl as he took her plump hand in his.

The other passengers stood in a tight little group, muttering to each other and looking furtively at the windows of the house. The two footmen were dressed in Neville livery, the girls wore country clothes but each carried a bundle, which I assumed to be their black dresses and aprons. Norbury strode out into the yard. He was impeccably turned out in black satin breeches, hose and jacket, the whitest of white ruffled shirts and with a neatly tied stock at his neck. He picked up Cook's bag and thrust it at one of the footmen.

'Come on, all of you!' he snapped. 'Get inside! There's work to be done!' Turning to Cook he inclined his head and said, gently, 'If you please, Mistress.'

The small group moved towards the door. There were smiles on their faces now and the girls chattered excitedly to each other. They were happy; they were home.

Norbury turned to Sergeant Finch.

'Now, if you would be so kind as to take this smelly cart out of my courtyard . . . '

'I'm going, I'm going,' Finch called out good-naturedly, and taking hold of the cart-horse's bridle he turned the big animal around to face the gatehouse archway. The smile left his face when he saw me standing there.

'Ah! Master Thomas, sir,' he called out. 'The Colonel asked me to stop off at the vicarage and pick up Master Giles, but I'm sorry to report your brother felt unable to come.'

This was so unlike my little brother, that it worried me. 'What reason did he give for not coming?' I asked.

201

The old Sergeant walked the horse and cart forward, only stopping when he was close enough to talk without shouting.

'He says the vicar is greatly upset and he feels he should stay with him, sir. Apparently the Reverend Hulse was riding back home across the heath and spied a fresh body in the gibbet. When he goes closer to say a prayer for the condemned man's departed soul he saw it was Ben Sorrel.'

'I don't believe it!' I exclaimed. 'A man's life forfeit for stealing a brace of rabbits or a few trout. Why in God's name wasn't I informed about his trial?'

'There weren't no trial, sir. Sorrel was murdered. There's no doubt about that. His throat was cut long afore he was put in that gibbet.'

He came even closer, lowering his voice to a hushed whisper. 'And it's my belief that them young men what calls themselves the Bucks' Club, knows something about it. Ben was a fool to spend so much of his time up at the priory a'spying on them no-good bastards — if you'll pardon my language, sir.'

With a click of his tongue and a gentle tug on the big horse's bridle, he led the horse out of the courtyard.

At least Hagar was happy. The silly dog ran behind the cart, leaping about like a spring lamb, emitting little yelps of pleasure.

As the heavy wagon cleared the gatehouse archway a string of riders was revealed, approaching the bridge at a brisk trot. In the gathering gloom I could just make out that it was my uncle leading them closely followed by a slim, upright figure that I presumed was Tobias. Next came a rider leading a pair of packhorses. That would be Corporal Prescott, the colonel's batman, and following him were two men wearing unfamiliar livery. Were these the flunkeys who had so impressed Prescott? Whoever they were, horsemen they most certainly were not, and no doubt cursing my uncle for setting such a spine-jolting pace.

I hurried forward to meet them. Sergeant Finch must have had the same idea as by the time I arrived on the scene the old cavalryman was holding both my uncle's and Tobias's steaming horses while Hagar ran round in circles beneath them, barking excitedly.

The colonel gave me a cheery wave and Tobias yelled, 'My dear Thomas! It's good to see you again.'

He saw me staring at the flunkeys who, with much cursing and grumbling, were getting down slowly and painfully from their horses.

'You remember Coggins and Fowler, of

course?' he said with a grin,

At the mention of their names, the two men slid to the ground and stood side by side, rigidly to attention. There was a wide smile on Fowler's weasel-like face and even Coggins' ugly mug sported a flickering lopsided grin.

I was delighted to see them and I shook them both warmly by the hand.

Tobias went on: 'With the jewels they 'liberated' from the pirate captain, these gentlemen bought themselves out of the Company's army. When they got to London, they went to the East India Company's offices to look for work. That is where Robert found them.'

Archie Fowler touched a knuckle to his forehead. 'Begging your pardon, Lieutenant, but General Clive says you're in some sort of trouble, so Dan and me asked if we could come along with Master Bloom and help out like.'

Coggins butted in. 'Life could do with a bit of livening up at the moment, sir, if you know what I mean. Archie and me are up for anything.' He then thought for a moment, and giving his mount a sideways look, added, 'So long as it doesn't mean a lot of this horse riding lark.'

My uncle cleared his throat. 'Master

Neville may have been a lieutenant in the Company's militia,' he said, 'but here in England he is a major in the King's army.'

Fowler's face reddened. 'I meant no disrespect, Major,' he said.

I smiled to put the little man at ease. 'You weren't to know,' I said. And then, to Tobias: 'While we are on the subject of rank, did I hear Fowler call Clive 'General' just now?'

He laughed. 'That's just a nickname they've given him at East India House, but these fellows seem to take it seriously. He sends you his compliments, Thomas. He was sorry he couldn't come himself and insisted I use his elegant coach. No one could get me here quicker than Hatton, he said. He sent the other two thinking they may prove useful to you.'

Remembering the fate that had befallen poor Ben Sorrel, I suggested we use them as a picquet. The last thing I wanted was to have Edwin Cruikshank, or any of his murderous friends turning up at the hall before I was ready for them. I asked if they were armed.

'We've both got pistols, Major,' Fowler replied. 'But I seen muskets on that pack horse.'

'A pistol apiece will be armament enough,' I said, smiling at the eager little cockney. 'I'd like you to stay here at the gatehouse. No one is to come in without my permission. Is that understood?'

Fowler knuckled his forehead again. 'You can rely on us, sir,' he said. 'Come on, Dan. Leave them nags to those as is used to 'em, you and me is on sentry go.'

Sergeant Finch and Corporal Prescott led the horses away and I took Tobias and my uncle across the courtyard to the house. I was well pleased with Norbury for he had all his footmen and housemaids smartly dressed and lined up at the hall porch to meet us. The house was more like its old self again with our Norbury back in charge.

My father was waiting for us in the great hall. When I saw him last he had been desperately in need of a shave and a clean shirt but now he was immaculately turned out in crisp, snow-white linen, a spotless beige waistcoat with topcoat and breeches in a rich, dark green material. His hose was black as were his shoes, which had buckles so bright, they dazzled your eyes. I did not have far to look for an explanation for this transformation for standing behind him, with a wide grin on his round face, was my batman, Lance Corporal Nolan.

'Sir Rupert did not appear to have a valet, sir,' he whispered. 'So I took it upon myself to assist the gentleman. I trust that meets with your approval, sir.'

My father took hold of my arm. 'Your man here tells me we have guests for dinner,' he said a trifle agitatedly. 'I do wish your mother wouldn't spring these things on me . . . Where is she, Thomas? She should be here to meet our visitors.'

Uncle Reuben brushed past me to embrace his brother. This reunion was difficult enough for him without having an audience so I backed away taking Tobias with me. A footman was standing like a statue by the fireplace holding a silver tray, upon which were several small glasses, filled with what I assumed was sherry, we both took one.

Tobias held his glass up to the light peering at the amber liquid as if it were a crystal ball. 'Now that I'm back in London I find I miss those gentle, well-mannered people of India, Thomas,' he said wistfully.

He sipped his drink and I tasted mine. I was right; it was a fine Amontillado.

'Well, have you sold it?' I asked eagerly.

'Of course.'

'How much did it bring? Is there enough to pay off my father's debt?'

'My dear fellow. Your stone made enough money to pay off the National Debt. You, sir, are an exceedingly wealthy man.'

The ringing of a gong, indicating that

dinner was served, prevented me from asking him just how much I was now worth.

★ ★ ★

There were only four of us dining, so the round table in the parlour had been set. I must say I felt decidedly uncomfortable to be entering my mother's favourite room and not having her there with us.

Norbury was standing in the doorway and as I passed him he whispered, 'I can honestly say, sir, that I have never encountered such a dearth of provisions. There was no meat, sir, no meat at all!'

I had a vision of us sitting down to bread and cheese or perhaps some of my father's chicken soup. There must have been a note of desperation in my voice when, out of the corner of my mouth, I said, 'But you've managed *something*, Norbury?'

He drew himself up to his full height and replied in that haughty voice all butlers use when they need to put their employers in their place, 'But of course, sir. Dinner today is *Ragout of Hare*.' He then went on to explain. 'The stable lad had caught a young leveret, sir, which, as you know, to be eaten in perfection should hang for several days, but before you could say 'knife', Cook had it cut into neat joints and simmering nicely in a little chicken stock with some strips of bacon . . . I took the liberty of adding a glass of port wine, sir — to improve the flavour.'

Four places were set at the big round table. I sat down opposite my poor bewildered father with Uncle Reuben to my left and Tobias to my right. The two brothers were deeply engrossed in conversation and from what I could overhear, Uncle Reuben seemed to be describing the benefits of a medical establishment in Chester while my father was more interested in learning when his younger brother would be going back to school.

I tucked into the hare, which, with red currant jelly and a mouth-watering selection of roast and boiled vegetables, proved to be a culinary treat. I felt sorry for Tobias who, because of the inclusion of bacon in the recipe, had to be content with only the vegetables.

Further testimony to Norbury's good housekeeping skills was that all the rooms had been aired, beds made up and fires lit in the grates. My guests were therefore able to stay in comfort at Dunmere Hall instead of facing a cold and tedious journey back to Napper's tavern.

The next day was Sunday. As morning service in the family chapel had been

discontinued during Cruikshank's administration we breakfasted late, played cards until
luncheon and then (having placed my father
in the Orangery under the watchful eye of the
singularly unobtrusive but ever attentive,
Nolan) we walked the fields with our guns.

All too soon our brief time together came
to an end. My uncle was due back with
his regiment and Tobias had business in
Manchester, so on our last evening together,
Norbury, who, as a result of some skilful
shooting that afternoon, had more game than
his larder could accommodate, served us with
rabbit soup, roast goose and a spiced fruit
concoction with a brandy sauce which, when
my uncle enquired after its name, was told it
was called, 'Hunter's Pudding'.

Giles had given me some idea of the size of
my father's debt, and the cost of building the
almshouses I already knew, so when Tobias
asked me how much money was needed to
put matters right, I simply added the two
amounts together. To me it seemed a colossal
sum and it took me completely by surprise
when he burst out laughing.

'My dear Thomas,' he said, wiping his eyes
on his napkin. 'You have no idea what that
diamond of yours was worth have you?' I
shook my head and Tobias, still chuckling,
said, 'You, sir, are what envious people in the

City are now calling a 'nabob'.'

'What on earth's that?' I asked.

'A nabob, my dear fellow, is a European who has amassed a fortune in India.' He bent his head closer. 'I've taken the liberty of opening an account in your name at my banking-house. They are using the letter you wrote to me as a specimen of your handwriting and signature, so all you need do now is give the creditor a note specifying the amount to be paid, sign it and tell him to present it at the bank. They will then pay him the money. Simple isn't it?' Then he whispered how much I had in this bank account. I must have looked dazed because he said, gently, 'Don't worry about it, Thomas. Just think of it as having enough money to pay off everything your father owes, finish building those little houses for the poor and still be quite comfortably off.'

After dinner, we gathered around the fireplace with pipes of good Virginia tobacco and a few bottles of Oporto's finest and talked late into the night.

★ ★ ★

The following morning, Nolan came to see me just after breakfast. Although still dressed in civilian clothes he stood to attention in the approved military manner. I noticed, however, that his fingers were playing nervously with the seams of his trousers.

'The colonel has given me leave to stay on here with you, sir,' he began.

'And you would rather return to barracks?'

He looked pained. 'Oh, no, sir!' he said. 'That's not it, that's not it at all.'

'Well, out with it, man. You either want to stay or you don't.'

'It's your father, sir,' he blurted out. 'The colonel has persuaded him to go to this doctor friend of his for a month or so, and seeing as you've got a house full of servants and he hasn't anyone to look after him . . .'

The man meant well and I smiled to put him at ease. 'All right, Corporal,' I said. 'You can accompany my father — so long as it's all right with the colonel!' He grinned and was about to leave when I added, 'For your information, Nolan . . .'

'Yes, sir?'

'This house is by no means full of servants.'

'No, sir.'

'And, Nolan!'

'Yes, sir?'

'Thank you.'

Tobias joined me in the courtyard just as the colonel's party were preparing to set off on their journey back to Chester.

212

My uncle heaved himself up into the saddle. 'A most successful operation, my boy,' he said, 'Keep in touch and let me know if there is anything else I can do. I know you won't be happy until Cruikshank is out of the county.'

Sergeant Finch had selected a docile-looking horse for my father who sat slumped in its saddle mumbling to himself. He seemed to be repeating the word, Cruikshank, over and over again. The name was obviously familiar to him and it was painful to watch him struggling to remember why. He suddenly perked up and I felt like cheering when he said with a grin, 'Lady Neville invited someone called Cruikshank to dinner once.'

★ ★ ★

Back in the great hall, Tobias announced cheerily, 'Well, it's me now, for the high road.'

'Sergeant Finch is going to miss, Hatton,' I said. 'Apparently he's doing a good job at the tavern.'

'That man seems to do a good job no matter what he's asked to do,' he said. 'For an old soldier he's an excellent coachman and you can see he enjoys driving a four-in-hand.'

He looked thoughtful for a moment and

then he said: 'I could leave Fowler at the tavern for a couple of days if you like. I'm sure that somewhere in that little man's murky past he must have worked in a hostelry.'

I was still having trouble with my conscience for having stolen Norbury away from Napper's Farm so I accepted this offer without hesitation. 'Finch was only here for the weekend,' I said. 'So he will go with you to collect your carriage. He'll be only too pleased to show Fowler the ropes.'

Tobias smiled and said, 'Right, that's settled then. I'll collect him on my way back south.'

After an early luncheon of rabbit pie and ale I found myself back in the courtyard once again, this time to see Tobias' party off the premises. The young merchant was mounted on the big stallion that had brought him to Dunmere Hall. The other horses from Josh Napper's stable were firmly tied to the back of the farm's cart in which Coggins and Fowler sat looking relieved to be passengers on this trip.

11

A fire had been lit in my father's study. I took off my coat and sat down at his desk.

I began by flipping through the thick ledgers that lay on its broad surface. These were big, heavy tomes with fine tooled-leather covers. Their content related to the estate but my father had not made the most recent entries. I knew his hand well. It was heavy and bold. He would blunt a point so quickly that when he was a magistrate his clerk was chosen as much for his dexterity with a penknife as for his legal knowledge. These later records were all written in a neat, flowing hand, almost like a woman's. These were Ashley's notes and, no doubt, the books were too big to fit in his portmanteau.

I flipped through the pages, finding lists of all sorts of things, from rents collected to an inventory of the contents of the house. I shuddered to read Ashley's cold and impersonal valuation of the things that had been loved and cherished by my family for generations. It could only have been compiled for one reason, to sell them.

Angrily, I snapped the ledger shut and

opened another. This time I found what I was looking for, a record of my father's creditors in date order, the earliest debt being the first. I knew it would be an accurate listing for if there was one thing I could rely on, it was Jacob Ashley's meticulousness with regard to money.

Full marks to my little brother though; his estimate wasn't all that far from the architect's total which was neatly underlined at the bottom of the column.

★ ★ ★

I applied myself to the task of visiting my father's creditors and it took me the best part of three weeks riding the length and breadth of the county to work my way down Ashley's list. Any discomfort I may have felt from so many hours in the saddle was far outweighed by the pleasure and satisfaction in seeing a look of surliness, or in some cases downright hostility, turn to one of surprise, or even gratitude, when I settled an account.

It was a crisp, sunny morning when I arrived at Holmes Chapel. There had been a sharp frost overnight and there was ice on the little stream that ran through the village. I was sheltered from the cold wind by the tall roadside hedges, the birds were singing and the sun on my face was pleasantly warm. I was in such good humour that I ventured to call on Jacob Ashley. The only thing I had left to do was get my father's almshouses finished and Ashley was, after all, a competent architect — and the only one this side of Manchester.

His clerk showed me into a dismal office that smelled strongly of mildew and mice. The man himself was seated behind a desk strewn with papers, most of which were rolled up, tied with ribbon and covered in dust.

'Master Neville!' he gasped and then, having got over his initial surprise he quickly corrected himself by saying, '*Major* Neville. Please forgive me, sir.'

He slid from behind the desk, the epitome of servility and, producing a large handker-chief of dubious cleanliness, began dusting down the only other chair in the miserable little room.

'To what do I owe the honour of this visit?' he lisped.

Remembering how bumptious he was in my father's office, it was quite satisfying to see him so humble in his own.

'The almshouses, Master Ashley. I take it you still have the plans?'

'Indeed I do, sir. Do you wish to see them?'

I declined to sit on the freshly dusted chair.

I was prepared to be civil but nothing more.

'No, I do not,' I said. 'I simply wish to know if you are prepared to complete the project.'

There was no humbug this time. The architect clasped his hands together and for a moment his eyelids closed as if in silent prayer. 'My dear sir,' he said at length. 'I would be delighted . . . and greatly obliged.'

Maintaining my hostility in the face of his almost painful gratitude was becoming a strain. 'Well, get on with it then,' I snapped, 'and send the bills to me.'

'I'll hire labour straight away, Major, and you will have my projected costs and an estimated completion date within two days.'

As I was leaving, he made me feel really mean by adding, 'May I thank you, sir, most sincerely on behalf of my wife and my children.'

'Just see you stick to my father's original concept,' I said, and I fled from the smelly little room.

★　★　★

I made Napper's Farm my next stop. I was in desperate need of some convivial company. Old Simon met me in the yard.

'That wind is bitter cold, Master Neville,'

he grumbled. 'It don't do my joints no good at all it don't.'

Oh, well, perhaps I could wait a moment or two for the friendly welcome, and Napper's Farm wouldn't be the same without old Simon and his grumbles. I dismounted and handed him the reins.

'Has my brother been in?'

'I haven't seen His Reverence for days, sir . . . Not even to borrow the cart.'

The old ostler will insist on giving Giles that rather grand title and each time I hear it I have to force myself not to laugh. I was still smiling when I said, 'You really shouldn't call him that. It isn't correct you know, and anyway, he hasn't even been ordained yet.'

Old Simon's wrinkled face lit up. 'Ah, but he soon will be,' he said smugly. 'Next Sunday it is. We got the Bishop coming and everything!'

I left the stables and headed for the taproom. So, my little brother's ordination had been arranged. Well, I was glad I was back in time to keep my promise to be there.

Archie Fowler was busily brushing the floor as I walked in. He looked up. 'Well, Major, you're a sight for sore eyes and no mistake!' he said, his narrow face split by a wide, toothy grin. He disappeared behind the row of barrels, quickly re-emerging tying a long white apron around his waist. 'What can I get you, sir, ale or wine, or perhaps something a bit stronger to keep the cold out?'

I opted for ale and settled myself into the inglenook. The fire was burning well, the pleasant, resinous smell from the logs proof they were cut from a pine tree.

'You seem quite at home here, Fowler,' I commented when he brought me my tankard.

The little cockney was still grinning. 'I likes this sort of work, Major. I spent a lot of my time in the army working in the canteens.' He looked wistfully around the taproom. 'I wouldn't mind having a place like this myself one day.'

I was still thinking about Giles. Perhaps Finch would know why he had not been to the tavern. Even if his romance with Megan Griffith was over it wasn't like my little brother to deny himself a tankard or two. I asked if the old sergeant was around.

'No, sir. He's up at the hall helping your butler to recruit more staff.' He sniggered behind his hand. 'Finch, a Recruiting Sergeant. I never thought of that before.' Then, suddenly remembering who he was talking to, he stood to attention and said, 'Don't misunderstand me, Major. The Sergeant's a good sort. He leaves me to run this place on my own and I respect him for that.'

I smiled. 'Relax, Fowler, you're not in the army now. And believe me, Sergeant Finch wouldn't leave you in charge of the tavern if you didn't have his respect also.'

A couple of drovers came in and Fowler went off to serve them. I finished my ale and left.

★ ★ ★

There had been a funeral at St Luke's. The mourners in their best Sunday clothes were just leaving the churchyard, the men grim-faced and the women silently weeping. Their next stop would be Josh's tavern and I was pleased to have avoided such doleful company.

I passed Jed Colclough, the wheelwright, walking his horse and cart back to his workshop. In addition to cartwheels, Jed made coffins, and for a fee he would also convey the departed to the church. He raised a finger to his forehead.

'Good day, Master Thomas,' he called out cheerfully. I asked him if my brother was at the church. 'No, sir, only the vicar. I heard him tell the churchwarden that Master Giles is 'in retreat'.' He scratched his head. 'Now what would that mean, sir?'

I smiled. 'It's nothing to worry about, Jed.

It's customary for someone about to be ordained to withdraw to a quiet place beforehand. Did the Reverend Hulse by any chance say where that might be?'

Jed brightened. 'He did that, sir, he said Master Giles is in retreat at the priory.'

★ ★ ★

It was dusk as I crossed the heath. Ahead I could just make out the twisted chimneys of Dunmere Hall silhouetted against the evening sky above the trees at the edge of the moorland. To my left stood the ruined façade of the priory, shining a ghostly grey in the twilight. I turned my horse towards the priory. Away in the distance a dog howled.

At the edge of the moor I urged my mount carefully through the belt of trees until I arrived at the priory's ivy-clad walls. This was my first sight of the old building since Jacob Ashley had made it habitable and from what I could see in the fast fading light, he'd made a good job of it. I was relieved to see that the recent additions had been made in sympathy with the ancient building. A great hall had been constructed with buttresses and gargoyles and tall stained-glass windows and although the stonework stood out as being new it had been carefully dressed to match the original so that in just a few years time, when the ivy had spread and it was covered in lichens and mosses, someone standing where I was now could be forgiven for classing the whole as being of the same age.

A baleful light shone through the windows and from within I could hear someone chanting a litany and many voices responding in unison. It was quite beautiful although somewhat spoiled by the occasional feminine giggle. I dismounted at a flight of wide stone steps that lead up to a heavy, wooden door. There was an inscription chiselled into the lintel above it. It was neither English nor Latin, *Fais ce que voudras*, it read, which my schoolboy French told me was something like, 'Do as you wish' or, perhaps more accurately, 'Do what you will'. To the side of the door was a bell-pull. I tugged on its big metal ring and was rewarded by a distant jangling noise from somewhere deep inside the building. After what seemed to be an age there was the sound of bolts being drawn.

The door opened to reveal a tall figure holding a lantern aloft which made his gaunt face appear even more ghoulish. I had rather expected to see Mandrake. He showed no surprise at seeing me either.

'The Master is not receiving,' he said, in his hollow, tomblike voice.

He was about to shut the door in my face so I jammed my booted foot in the gap. 'I am here to see my brother,' I said determinedly.

He retreated into the building leaving me staring down a narrow passageway that had a flagstone floor and wood panelled walls. The darkness inside made it impossible to assess how far it extended into the building but when the manservant's light reappeared it was a good ten yards away. Arriving at the door, he stood to one side to allow my little brother to squeeze past him. Giles had a glass of wine in his hand and a silly grin on his face.

'What on earth brings you here, Tom?' he asked.

I steered him away from the door. 'I was told you'd gone into retreat.'

'I don't know where you got that rubbish from, old chap,' he said with a grin. 'Edwin Cruikshank invited me here.' He winked and nudged me with an elbow. 'And I've had a wonderful time. You should have been here, lots and lots to drink — and lots and lots of pretty girls!' He turned to go back in. 'Edwin says I can stay 'til my ordination, and I might just do that. So go home, Tom, and leave me be, there's a good fellow.' He raised his glass and winked again.

And for the very first time I saw a ghost of a smile on Mandrake's face.

On my way up the long drive to Dunmere Hall, I saw three men walking towards me who, when they saw me coming, stepped respectfully to the side of the road and doffed their hats. One I thought I recognised as having once been a gardener in our employ, the others I did not. Norbury was evidently engaging outside staff too.

When I got to the moat bridge the young stable lad was stationed there waiting to take my horse, and to my delight Hagar was with him. Sergeant Finch had done a good job on the boy during the short time he had been at the stables and I wondered what kind of mystical training he had given the lad to make his hearing as sharp as that of an old cavalryman.

'All you need is a dog, sir.' The lad said when I asked him. 'They know there's someone coming long before you hears 'em.'

I walked into the hall porch. There was no one around so I shouted a loud, 'Hallo!' I didn't have long to wait before I heard the sound of running feet.

Norbury appeared red in the face, as much from embarrassment as exertion. 'I *do* beg you pardon, sir,' he gasped. 'I was otherwise engaged and didn't hear your approach.'

'I think we will have to get more dogs, Norbury,' I said, hiding a smile behind my hand.

'Yes, sir,' he replied in the voice butler's use when their master is talking rubbish.

'I hear you have been engaging more staff,' I said. 'I must say I see very little evidence of them here.'

I could see that my remark startled him but he quickly regained his composure and in true Norbury style proceeded to take control of the situation.

'Benson, your father's bailiff, has returned, sir. I found him working at his brother's smithy. There really isn't sufficient work in the village for two smiths so he was delighted to know that you got rid of the fellow Master Ashley had put in his place. He'll be reporting to you shortly for your instructions.' He then coughed into his hand the way butlers do. 'As my duties are now rather more that of a house steward, sir,' he said somewhat haughtily. 'I have taken the liberty of appointing an under butler to wait at table ... I shall, of course, retain control of the wine cellar.' He shot me a challenging look. I shrugged my shoulders to indicate that I had no objection and he carried on. 'I have also taken on a laundry-maid, an under laundry-maid and a maid-of-all-work.'

'I passed three men on the way in,' I said. 'One of them used to work here as a gardener.'

'That would be Meadows, sir. I have actually engaged four gardeners and as Meadows knows his way around the grounds I've put him in charge. I had hoped to have Brownlow back as Head Gardener — Cook always said he grew the finest legumes and brassicas in the county — but sadly he passed away last September.'

'So is the household now up to strength?'

'There *is* the question of your valet, sir. I have a list of applicants for the position but no doubt you will wish to conduct the interviews yourself . . . And we will require personal servants for Sir Rupert and Lady Neville, when they take up residence here again.'

★　★　★

My room, although well lit with candles, felt like an ice well. This was apparently about to be rectified for no sooner had I stepped inside than a young girl appeared carrying a large wooden bucket containing logs and kindling. She placed the bucket on the floor and bobbed a curtsey.

'I, I, I been told to light a fire for you, sir,' she stuttered.

She was no beauty, just a simple, honest country girl and from her age and apparent nervousness I assumed this was her first job. This would no doubt be Master Norbury's new maid-of-all-work. I gave her an encouraging smile, but instead of getting on with her chore she just stood there with her head bowed, fiddling with the end of her sackcloth apron. After a long, agonising moment she spoke again.

'M, M, Master Newbury told me to say he's having a hipbath sent up for you, sir.'

Good old Newbury! The thought of soaking my aches and pains away in a tub of hot water was bliss. Once again I gave the old butler full marks for his unfailing attention to detail.

I looked with pity at the simple lass with her soot-streaked face. Heaven knows what she thought her news would have me do, strip off my clothes before her eyes perhaps. Having delivered her message, the girl threw herself into the task of lighting the fire and immediately the kindling bust into flame she fled, leaving her bucket standing on the hearth. Taking two of the logs from the bucket I threw them on the fire. Then, to give the room time to warm up, and for my bath to arrive, I wandered out into the gallery

I have never thought of myself as a

particularly religious person. I go to church on Sundays and say my prayers before going to sleep at night, because that was what I was brought up to do. Since Emily's disappearance, however, I have prayed fervently each and every day for her safety, and so, when I found myself outside the door to the chapel, I opened it and went inside. The place smelled damp and was quite dark, the only light coming through the ancient stained glass of the tall, pointed window behind the altar. But I had no need for illumination for I was on familiar ground.

The door from the gallery led onto a small balcony, comfortably furnished with upholstered pews. This is where the family and their guests would gather for Sunday worship, the floor of the chapel with its hard wooden benches being for the estate workers and other servants. Without being able to see it clearly I knew that to my right was a narrow stairway to the chancel enabling those in the balcony to descend and receive the sacrament at the altar rail.

I sat in one of the pews for a moment thinking about Emily, and praying that her father would find her safe and bring her home. Now that I had the means, I would join the search for her, just as soon as I had things sorted out at home.

There was a noise below. Good old Norbury, I thought, I bet he's sent someone to clean and air the place. God knows it could do with it! The damp coldness was beginning to penetrate my clothes and, judging that my room would have warmed up by now, I left the chapel and went to see if the bath had arrived.

When I opened the door I saw that a screen had been set up halfway across the room and between this and the fire stood a high-backed bath that was steaming nicely. The servants had gone, looking for me in all probability, so without more ado I hurriedly stripped off my clothes, stepped into the tub and eased my tired body down into the delightfully hot water. It was heaven!

In my haste to slip into the soothing waters I hadn't taken stock of where the towels and soap had been placed and, too late, I discovered they were well out of reach. I heard the door open and assuming it was Norbury or one of the footmen returning I called out to whoever it was to hand me the cake of soap.

It was a soft, husky, feminine voice that answered.

'Hello, soldier-boy,' it purred, and Megan Griffith sidled around the screen and stood looking down at me.

Acutely conscious of being as naked as the day I was born and that the water in which I sat was crystal clear, I shouted, 'For God's sake, woman, throw me a towel!'

She ignored me and proceeded to kneel down on the hearthrug beside the bath. 'Did you know that some people call me a witch?' she asked.

I drew my knees up and held them there by wrapping my arms around my legs. 'I have heard it said,' I grunted.

'My father died when I was a little girl,' she said, trolling a finger absently through the bath water. 'Here at Dunmere Hall.'

Now that *was* a surprise. 'Did he work here?' I asked.

'In a way,' she replied. 'He was a travelling cooper. He could make anything from barrels and buckets to butts and butter churns. We crossed the border because it was said there was plenty of work here but we didn't bargain for you English being so mistrustful of foreigners. We spoke very little of your language you see, and we would have starved if it hadn't been for Sir Rupert, he gave my father work and encouraged his tenants to do the same.'

'That sounds like my father and his 'good works',' I said.

She rose gracefully to her feet and glided

over to my chest of drawers upon which stood a pottery claret jug and some beakers. Picking up the jug she removed the cover and sniffed the contents. 'Want some?' she asked.

The fire needed making up and the bath water was going cold. So much for my luxurious soak I thought. 'No,' I replied grumpily. 'But I'd be grateful for a towel and my dressing gown.'

With a resigned shrug of her shoulders, she gathered up the items and tossed them onto the hearthrug where I could reach them. She then proceeded to pour herself some claret and while her back was turned I quickly got out of the bath and wrapped the towel around myself.

'You've got nothing I haven't seen before, soldier-boy.'

I'd forgotten the damned mirror! I grabbed my dressing gown and ducked behind the screen. 'You're a wicked woman, Megan Griffith,' I said.

'And you men like me all the better for it!' she replied with a toss of her head.

My dressing gown was a voluminous, quilted garment, and only when I had it wrapped tightly about my person and its sash securely tied did I feel able to leave the sanctuary of the screen. I threw another log on the fire with no immediate effect.

'I believe you enjoy your reputation of being Goostrey's wicked lady.'

'I don't give a damn what others think. I make more money in a week entertaining gentlemen than my poor old mother did in a whole year with her herbal remedies . . . and folk tend to leave you alone if they think you've got the evil eye.' She laughed again. 'Pretending to be a witch gives me better protection than the fiercest of guard dogs.'

When she poured herself some more claret I noticed that her hand was shaking a little. 'I never thought it would attract the real thing,' she said.

'The real thing?'

She looked up. 'That damned Satanist, Edwin Cruikshank.'

As much as I hated to come to that odious man's defence I couldn't help reminding her that he was, after all, an ordained priest.

'A priest he may be,' she said, 'but have you ever seen him step on consecrated ground?' She laughed roguishly. 'When he was the estate manager here, your chapel was one of the few places where Giles and I could meet in complete safety.'

'But I'm told he celebrates mass at the priory.'

'That he does, soldier-boy, but *his* candles are black!'

She joined me at the fireplace. My recent addition to the room's source of heat was now producing a great amount of smoke.

'You were right,' she said. 'He did call me his sister. He believed we were both serving the same master you see.' She bent forward and taking up a poker from the hearth she prodded the log, producing a flurry of sparks that mingled with the smoke. 'Oh, I was happy to play along,' she said with a derisive laugh. 'I'd never had such high-class trade.' Standing up, she grasped my hand and looked at me beseechingly. 'Promise me you will get Giles away from the priory,' she begged. 'Edwin is a sick man. Each day his coughing gets worse. He's very weak and he's coughing up blood. He can't have much longer to live.'

'What has that got to do with my brother?'

She released my hand and stared back at the fire. 'Because Edwin says he's immortal,' she whispered

'He's what?'

She turned on me, her eyes flashing. 'Immortal, deathless, lives forever! God damn it, soldier-boy, don't make me repeat myself!'

There was obviously more to come so I said nothing and waited until she was ready to continue. I didn't have to wait very long.

'He asked me once to guess how many

women he'd had. Can you believe that?'

I tried to look suitably incredulous.

'He then went on to tell me that in this lifetime, this lifetime, mark you, he must have had hundreds.'

'The cad!'

'Then came the frightening part. He said that being as old as time itself, he must have had thousands upon thousands.'

She shuddered and without thinking I put my arm around her.

'In my profession you hear a lot of rubbish talked in bed,' she went on. 'God knows I'm not a religious woman, but being near that man troubles my very soul.'

This was just nonsense, wasn't it? I forced a laugh. 'Edwin Cruikshank is a charlatan, madam!' I said. 'How can someone possibly be as old as time?'

She looked at me very seriously. 'I can't believe I asked him that, but I did,' she said. 'He told me he's a traveller and the body he inhabits is nothing more than a vehicle which, when it wears out or he gets tired of it, he swaps for another.'

The horror of the scenario struck me. 'You mean he's got designs on, on Giles's body?'

'Well, what do you think?' she said, slipping out from under my arm. 'With his present body dying on him what better to replace it with than a fit young man just about to be ordained into the Church ... Edwin likes being a priest, he says it adds 'savour', whatever that means.'

She went back to the claret jug and this time I asked her to pour one for me. God knows I needed a drink after all that!

'Don't ask me what Edwin's planning to do,' she said, 'but whatever it is, it's going to happen right after your brother's ordination.'

12

You dream every night, they say. Well, if that is so, mine must evaporate in the morning sun like the dew on the grass, as in my case they are forgotten the moment I awake. Last night however, was the exception.

There I was, slogging it out on a moonlit milling field with a monster that to begin with was an exceedingly tall Cruikshank but who, as the bout progressed, gradually metamorphosised into Lucifer himself complete with horns and tail. We fought in a ring formed by dozens of drunken young men in monk's habits, waving flaming torches and baying for blood.

I hadn't thought of Hari Lal since I left India but there he was, in my corner, waving his skinny brown arms and shouting, 'Beware the blade, *sahib*! Beware the blade!' and as the devil and I traded blows, I wondered where a stripped-to-the-waist, bare-knuckle fighter could hide a knife?

★ ★ ★

Later, when I was standing outside the hall porch hoping the fresh air would clear my head and perhaps help me to make sense of the dream, a sudden clatter of hooves and the echoing rumble of ironbound wheels startled me. Shielding my eyes from the glare of the morning sun I was delighted to see Robert Clive's magnificent carriage framed in the gatehouse arch.

Hagar's barking and the shouts from the coachman brought Norbury scurrying into the courtyard, immediately followed by two footmen and a gaggle of housemaids — although, on second thoughts, 'giggle' would perhaps be a better collective noun to describe our female household servants.

The old butler (or should I think of him now as my steward?) pushed and prodded his staff into a line in front of the hall porch entrance, with urgent whispered instructions to fasten a button here and straighten a pinafore there, before setting off with unhurried dignity to open the carriage door.

Tobias leapt down and shook me warmly by the hand. 'I'm very impressed by the guard of honour,' he said, nodding at the line-up. 'But you look like death, old chap. Have a heavy night did we?'

I was well awake now and delighted to see the young Jewish merchant again, doubly so as he was just the man to help me with what I had in mind. His driver gave me a smart salute with his whip.

'Pleased to see you again, sir,' he called down from the box. 'Company Sergeant Major Hatton, sir.'

'Late of the Royal Welch Fusiliers,' I shouted back with a laugh.

'*And* The East India Company Militia, sir.'

★ ★ ★

Norbury shouted instructions for Tobias's things to be taken to the guest suite and then followed me as I showed my visitor into the great hall. A straight-faced, middle-aged man appeared carrying a silver salver, upon which rested a bottle of brandy and some glasses. He set the tray down carefully on the long refectory table.

'Smallwood, sir, the new under butler,' Norbury whispered to me out of the corner of his mouth. I waited for him to retire before pouring Tobias and myself a large one.

'It's good to see Hatton again,' I said. 'But where's Coggins?'

'Hatton was anxious to see how Fowler was managing at the tavern and asked if we could stop there briefly on our way here — and it was a good thing we did, they were run off their feet! So I left Coggins there to help out.'

We gravitated to the warm cheerfulness of the fireplace where Tobias proceeded to stretch his back and flex his legs. 'Can't do with being cooped up in a damned carriage, Thomas,' he said. 'Give me a good horse between my legs any day.' He stopped his exercises to peer at me quizzically. 'You look a bit worried, is everything all right?'

I related in detail my conversation with Megan Griffith, leaving nothing out — except for being in the bath at the time.

'That's a rum do and no mistake,' he said when I had finished. 'Do you believe her?'

I placed my glass on the high mantelshelf and stood with the fingertips of both hands clutching the edge of the massive beam and stared down into the fire.

'I've mulled this over in my mind until my head is spinning,' I said. 'God knows Megan's relationship with Giles is out of the ordinary, to say the least but I can see no other reason for her coming to me with such a bizarre story.'

He thought for a moment and then he beamed at me. 'My dear old chap,' he said. 'I don't believe any of this mumbo-jumbo, but from what you say, this fellow Cruikshank is on his last legs. Consumption is it?'

I nodded in agreement.

'Well, the answer's as plain as a pikestaff,

old boy. All you have to do is make sure your brother is well out of the way when he breathes his last, and then, with no one to jump into, this demon or evil spirit or whatever it is will jolly well have to expire with him, eh, what?'

He laughed, but I didn't join in.

'Come on, cheer up. I tell you what. I'll bet you my gold watch to your dog, Hagar, that there isn't a grain of truth in this nonsense . . . Giles gets ordained tomorrow, you say?'

'Yes, right after Matins.'

'There were a lot of carriages at the tavern. The ostler said some club or other is meeting at the priory this weekend. Has that got something to do with all this?'

That was all I needed. We could deal with Mandrake and any other servants Cruikshank may have up there, but it would be another matter if the place were full of his supporters.

'It's the Bucks Club,' I said miserably. 'They're a bunch of dissolute young rakes who enjoy dressing up as monks and indulge in all sorts of wickedness from orgies to the Black Mass, depending on whose story you listen to.'

There are times in life when an idea pops into your mind from goodness knows where and you know immediately that it's the very solution you've been racking your brains to find.

'We don't wait until tomorrow!' I announced. 'It's customary for the ordinand, that's Giles, to spend the night before the ceremony in solitary prayer, you know, like a squire about to be knighted keeping vigil over his armour. Now where is he going to do that? If Megan Griffith is right about Cruikshank's abhorrence of anything sanctified I very much doubt if the priory chapel has been re-consecrated, so that only leaves St Luke's church. We should have the perfect opportunity to snatch Giles there.'

'But what about the ceremony? Won't he be rather put out to miss it, with the Bishop coming and everything?'

I think Tobias was surprised when I laughed at that. 'Giles is not really cut out to be a priest,' I said. 'He's only acting the part to please my mother. I think my little brother will be grateful to be got off the hook ... Shall we say dawn tomorrow then?'

'I beg your pardon?'

'Dawn, Tobias, daybreak! The hour when our quarry, having been awake all night, will be at his lowest ebb. Whereas you and I, having had a good night's sleep, will have all our wits about us.'

'Whoa! Just hold on a moment,' he said.

242

'This is your little brother we're talking about, not a French regiment from Pondicherry.'

'A regiment or one person, the time to go in is at dawn, believe me, I know, my best friend's a general,' I said, and we both laughed.

★ ★ ★

We set off in the estate wagon well before daybreak, and as the first glimmer of light appeared in the eastern sky we were in St Luke's churchyard carefully picking our way between the graves. In the distance I could hear a faint twittering as the birds in the hedgerows began to stir, but over the ancient burial ground there hung a brooding silence. The night had been overcast with cloud so there was no frost, but a grey mist blanketed the ground obscuring some of the smaller headstones. I stubbed my toe a few times and somewhere over to my left I could hear Tobias cursing under his breath.

Suddenly, the stillness was shattered by the piercing shriek of an owl and at that same moment a shadowy figure slipped out of the church and vanished into the swirling mist.

There was a muffled cry, a triumphant shout, and then Tobias called, 'Quickly! Over here, Thomas, I've got one of them!'

I slipped and slid across the moss-covered graves, and there he was, gleefully sitting on top of someone dressed in a long, hooded monk's habit. My companion may be slim but he was no lightweight and had his prisoner well and truly pinned to the ground.

'This must be one of your Bucks' Club people, Thomas,' he shouted. 'He's a scrawny young devil. If they're all like this one we shouldn't have any trouble.'

A muffled female voice came from within the hood.

'Damn your eyes, soldier-boy! Get this heavy lump off me!'

Oh, my God! I should have known my little brother wouldn't face the long hours of the night on his own, if he could help it.

'Let her up, Tobias,' I said with a sigh. 'It's Megan Griffith.'

He grudgingly got off Megan's back and she stood up brushing down the front of her long hooded robe.

'The next time you feel the need to ride me, sir, I trust you'll chose a more comfortable situation,' she said scornfully, and then turning to me, added, 'Giles is quite alone, soldier-boy. Sorry, got to go, call of nature,' and with that she slipped away between the gravestones.

Leaving Tobias gawping after her, I entered the church alone. Apart from two candles burning on the altar the place was in darkness. The icy coldness of the stone-flagged floor and bare walls began to chill me through to the skin. A tentative enquiry of, 'Giles are you there?' brought no response. Conscious that my voice had been nothing more than a reverent whisper induced by my surroundings I tried again, only louder this time. 'Giles, it's me, Tom!'

The door of the vestry burst open flooding the little church with light, and there was my brother framed in the doorway, a glass of wine in one hand and a half eaten chicken leg in the other.

'What on earth!' he began and then he grinned. 'You look absolutely frozen, old boy. For goodness sake come in here. I've got the stove going and it's red-hot, halfway up the flue.'

It was so hot in the small room I was forced to remove my coat. The dozens of candles he had burning in there would have been sufficient to keep the place warm but added to that the little charcoal stove was glowing cherry red in the corner. It was like stepping back into the dry heat of India.

'Megan brought me some, er'um,' Giles cleared his throat. 'Some home comforts.'

'Yes, I met her outside,' I said. There was no time to beat about the bush. 'Look Giles, you've got to come home with me, right now.'

He was taken aback by my suggestion but I got the impression he wasn't entirely opposed to it. 'But what about my ordination?' he ventured.

At that moment Megan chose to return, followed by Tobias. He looked a little apprehensive. It occurred to me that perhaps he'd never been inside a Christian church before.

'Damn your ordination,' Megan said. 'What the hell do you want to be a priest for anyway?'

Giles bristled at that. 'We've had this out before, Meg,' he said, 'and my answer is still the same. I grant you the only reason I went away to study for the priesthood in the first place was to please my mother, but I've worked hard at it and I've had to put up with all sorts of hardship. Now it's within my reach I'm going to damn well take it. I've earned it!' He went over to the stove and stood with his back to the rest of us silently drinking his wine.

Tobias shot me an enquiring look. I shrugged my shoulders. I didn't know what to do. I could hardly tap my little brother on the head, could I?

'Mother would be heartbroken,' Giles mumbled to himself. He wiped away a tear and I got the impression he'd had more than one glass of wine that night. 'And Edwin would be disappointed.' He turned around to face us. 'D'you know, Tom,' he said, swaying ever so slightly. 'I think that man loves me . . . no, no, you can smile, but whenever I'm near him he looks at me all doe-eyed and nods his head approvingly like I'd just ridden the winner in the Knutsford Gold Cup. He likes to touch me as well, feel my muscles, that sort of thing. If he wasn't such a lecher I'd think he was one of those . . . well, you know.'

Megan brushed past me and taking the empty glass from his hand, said, 'Here, Giles. Let me get you another drink.'

'By the look of it, I'd say he's had quite enough,' I began, but as the woman turned away from my brother she winked at me. She then busied herself at the picnic hamper and returned with the glass refilled.

'Have some, Tom . . . and your friend,' Giles said cheerfully. 'It's a good claret. Better than that watered down stuff old Hulse keeps for communion.' He drank deeply and wiped his mouth with the back of his hand. 'And there's plenty of fowl, or there's cheese if you prefer . . . ' His voice tailed off and his eyes glazed over. I stepped forward and caught him as his knees buckled. The glass fell from his hand and smashed to pieces on the stone floor.

I was surprised how heavy he was in my arms. Tobias helped me carry him outside and lay him on a back pew while Megan stayed in the vestry to sweep up the glass.

It was obvious that she must have slipped something in his drink as he was absolutely dead to the world. Near to panic, I called out, 'My God, woman! What have you given him?'

She came out and stood looking down at him with a smile on her face. 'Don't worry, soldier-boy,' she said. 'I wouldn't do anything to harm your brother. A few drops of laudanum that's all. After all the wine he's had, it will make him sleep like a baby.' She flashed me a wicked smile. 'I always carry some with me. It helps calm my more aggressive customers.'

Leaving Megan clearing up in the vestry, Tobias and I carried Giles out to the cart. An estate wagon is a light, four-wheeled vehicle with a bench seat for two people and sufficient carrying capacity in the back to take a couple of pigs to market or fetch in a goodly supply of logs. With Giles stretched out and sleeping peacefully behind us, we drove back to the Hall. For some reason we didn't talk, the only sounds during the journey were the rumble of the wheels on the rutted surface of the road and my brother's sonorous snoring.

The stable lad was at the bridge when we got there with Hagar bounding about and barking excitedly as usual. I told the boy to run on ahead and ask Norbury to meet us at the hall porch. As we passed through the gatehouse arch I could see the faithful old servant hurrying towards us closely followed by Smallwood and two footmen. I suppose, seeing Giles laying in the back of the cart, apparently unconscious, the lad had assumed he'd met with an accident.

Norbury hardly waited for the gig to stop. 'Get him inside, Smallwood,' he shouted. 'And send someone for Doctor Ramsay.'

'There's no need to bother the good doctor,' I said, jumping down and forcing a smile. 'All Master Giles needs is rest. Take him to his old room and put him to bed.'

The footmen lifted Giles out of the back of the wagon and to Smallwood's shouts of, 'Easy! Go easy with him,' and 'For God's sake, mind that step!' they carried him into the house.

'My brother has had a little too much wine,' I told Norbury when they were out of earshot. 'Put a large chamber pot by his bed and leave him to sleep it off.'

The stable lad climbed onto the wagon but instead of leaping in beside him, Hagar hesitated and stood eyeing me eagerly. I called her and she came bounding over, her tail wagging and her tongue lolling out with pleasure. The lad was about to drive off when Tobias stepped forward and stopped him. After exchanging a few words the young merchant took out a purse and pressed some coins into his hand. The boy grinned from ear to ear, touched his forehead in salute and drove off.

'What was all that about?' I asked.

'I sent him to fetch Coggins and Fowler. I thought we might need them to man the gatehouse again.'

'You had no need to pay him.'

'I didn't. I saw several monstrous hares hanging outside the butcher's shop in Goostrey yesterday. I know it won't be open today but I told the lad to go there anyway. I'm sure the butcher will be glad of a sale and it will please the lad's mother.' He smiled. 'Your man, Norbury, told me the story behind that excellent dinner he conjured up from nowhere the last time I was here.'

It was a gesture typical of Tobias. We walked towards the house.

'There'll be a hullabaloo when the bishop arrives at St Luke's for morning service,' I said. 'The first person he'll look for is my brother and when he discovers he's not there, all hell will break loose — if his lordship will pardon the expression.'

'From what you've told me, Cruikshank won't be at the church himself but I don't doubt he'll have his spies there,' Tobias added. 'And it won't take a genius to work out where Giles is, so we may well need that pair of ruffians.'

* * *

A fire was burning in the hearth in the great hall. I sent for some brandy and, having lit a pipe each, we sat with our chairs drawn right up to the fireplace and talked. Smallwood appeared to ask if we were ready to eat. I looked at the clock and was surprised to see it was almost noon.

'We will take luncheon late today, Smallwood,' I said, looking at my guest for his agreement. 'Shall we say two o'clock?' Tobias nodded.

Hagar was showing signs of wanting to go out so I took her to the hall porch. While I was waiting for her to return, the estate wagon rumbled into the courtyard with Sergeant Finch driving it. I guessed the two muffled figures in the back were Coggins and Fowler.

Following close behind were two riders. I recognised the stocky figure of Lance Corporal Nolan, the other, although somehow familiar I couldn't immediately place, for he wore a black tricorne hat pulled low over his eyes and a scarf was wrapped around the lower half of his face.

Finch raised his whip. 'Good day to you, sir,' he shouted gleefully. 'Got a nice surprise for you here.'

He halted the wagon a short distance away so that the two riders could bring their mounts close to the porch. With her needs satisfied, Hagar bounded back to perform her self-imposed duty of running between the animals' legs and barking at their hooves. Nolan reached forward in the saddle to take hold of the other bridle as the rider dismounted. The man in the black hat walked towards me unwinding the scarf from his face as he did so. I caught my breath. It was my father.

We stood looking at each other for a moment, neither of us knowing quite what to say. He looked well, or at least better than I remembered. Suddenly and without warning he stepped forward and clasped me in his arms. God! How I had longed for that when I was a child. When we parted we both had tears in our eyes.

I tried to swallow the lump in my throat. 'Welcome home, sir,' I said.

Tobias came out to see what all the commotion was about. Instantly recognising that this was a difficult moment for both my father and me, he went across to Finch and the two former Company soldiers who were standing in a group by the wagon. Smallwood had followed him out and stood at a respectful distance awaiting further instructions.

My father tilted his head in his direction. 'Who's he?' he whispered.

'That's Smallwood, he's the new butler.'

'The devil he is,' my father said thoughtfully. 'What happened to Norbury?'

Has he forgotten the sinister Mandrake, I wondered?

'I promoted him to steward,' I said, which was a lot simpler than saying Norbury had promoted himself.

He addressed the servant. 'There will be one more for luncheon, my good fellow . . . and tell cook to expect four more in the servant's hall.'

My father's redoubtable appearance could be quite frightening to someone who had never met him before and I could tell that Smallwood didn't want to offend either my important looking guest or me. He shot me a look of desperation.

'This is my father,' I said quickly, 'Sir Rupert Neville.'

I saw a look of relief on the new butler's face as his head dipped in a businesslike bow. 'Yes, Sir Rupert,' he said. 'Cook has prepared roast duck, sir. I trust that meets with your approval.'

'A promising fellow, that,' my father said as we followed Smallwood into the house. 'I suppose we've got that stuffy boor, Hulse, with us again for luncheon.'

He seemed to have forgotten that Cruikshank had stopped the Sunday services in our chapel, but before I could refresh his memory he put me in a difficult position by asking, 'Where's your mother, Thomas?'

This was a question I had been dreading. I was trying to decide whether to put off the evil moment by saying she was out or take the bull by the horns and tell him she had left home when a voice behind me whispered, 'You'll find Sir Rupert's memory of the past few weeks a bit hazy, Major.' It was Nolan. He stepped past me to go to my father. 'You'll meet everyone soon enough, sir,' he said to him gently. 'I've asked for some hot water to be sent to your room. I'll come up with you, sir, and lay out a clean shirt for luncheon.'

Nolan led the way up the stairs and my

father followed him like a lamb. Finding myself alone in the great hall, I wandered back out into the courtyard. There was no sign of Tobias so I assumed he'd gone to the gatehouse with Coggins and Fowler. The two horses were fastened to the back of the estate wagon ready to be taken to the stables, but for the moment Sergeant Finch was busy playing tug-of-war with Hagar. He became conscious of someone watching and looked up sheepishly.

'She's a grand dog, Master Thomas. I miss her.'

'How is it you are driving the estate wagon?' I asked. 'What happened to my stable lad?'

Finch laughed. 'He turned up at the tavern with a damned great rabbit, said it was for his mother. I told him to take it to her and I'd drive Dan and Archie over here.' Still grinning he looked at me for a moment and said, 'Don't you worry about the horses, Master Thomas. I'll see to 'em. I've got Ernie Goodrich's eldest daughter, Millie, helping out in the tavern. She's got a good head on her shoulders that one, so I don't have to rush back.'

Having inherited her father's stature, Millie Goodrich will have no problem keeping the drunks in order, I thought.

I left Sergeant Finch and Hagar growling at each other and made my way to the servants' hall. There was the usual commotion when I walked in and as usual I smiled and waved a proprietorial hand to signify that they should ignore me and get on with whatever they were doing. I made for the long table, Nolan had been sitting there but now he was on his feet and standing to attention. Soldiers on parade do not respond to a wave of the hand.

'At ease, Corporal,' I said. 'We can talk while you eat that roast duck, it looks delicious.'

'Thank you, Major.' He sat down and picked up a wing. The skin crackled between his teeth as he bit into it and the fat ran down his chin. 'It would be a sin to let such a well prepared bird get cold,' he said, obviously for Cook to hear.

'Tell me about my father,' I said. 'What did you mean about his memory being hazy?'

Nolan wiped his mouth on his napkin. 'The colonel's friend, Doctor Haas, you know, sir, the one who has the clinic. Well, he puts people to sleep by just talking to them.' He read the look on my face and said, 'No, it's true, sir. I've seen him do it. He just sits them down, tells them to think of nothing and talks to them quietly and in no time at all they're asleep. I was there when he did it to your father, sir.'

It sounded to me like something one would see at a travelling show, but here was Nolan telling me that my father, the most sceptical of sceptics, was 'talked' to sleep.

'What was the purpose of this demonstration,' I asked.

'Oh, it was no demonstration, sir, it was the cure, so it was. While Sir Rupert was asleep, the doctor told him to go back in his mind to a time before he needed the drink. And it worked, sir. It's a miracle, so it is. The colonel couldn't get over it. Forgetting the odd thing that happened in the last month or so is not much of a price to pay for that now, is it sir?'

I had to agree.

I left Nolan to finish his duck and went to find Coggins and Fowler. I dearly wanted my mother to be seated in her usual place at the big round table in the parlour when my father came down for luncheon, and I had about an hour to do it.

'I'm going to bring my mother home,' I announced, bursting into the gatehouse. 'And I could do with some help.'

Dan Coggins banged the table with his fist, causing the maid who had just brought another jug of ale from the kitchen to squeal and run out of the room.

'If it means a scrap, lead me to it,' he said. 'Life has been deadly dull of late.'

'You can say that again, Dan,' Fowler added. 'I take it you'll want us to bring our pistols, Major?'

'Yes, whatever weapons you have. Meet me on the moat bridge in ten minutes. All right?'

I ran to the stables where I began wheeling out the estate wagon.

'Best leave me to do that, sir.' It was Sergeant Finch. He looked at me inquisitively. 'If you care to tell me where it is you want to go, I'll be happy to drive you.'

'The old priory to bring Lady Neville home,' I shouted. 'It could be dangerous.'

Finch went to one of the stalls and brought out a strong-looking mare and began harnessing her to the wagon. 'I looked after you when you were a boy, Master Thomas. If you're about to ride into danger my place is still at your side.'

The two former Company soldiers were waiting at the bridge. The estate wagon rumbled to a stop. 'Right lads, up you get,' Finch shouted.

'Wait for me, Sergeant!' A short, sturdy figure came running from the house carrying an assortment of swords, a variety of powder horns and an ancient blunderbuss that looked positively lethal to anyone fool enough to go anywhere near it. 'I gathered these up from around the house when the maid told us what you were up to,' Nolan said with a grin.

Willing hands helped him into the wagon and we rumbled off at a trot for the old priory.

13

Leaving the estate wagon out of sight in the wood, we moved forward in a line abreast as silent as ghosts, our footsteps muffled by the thick carpet of leaves. The only sounds were of an occasional fluttering of a bird high up in the branches and the faint Gregorian chant wafting across from the new basilica.

I had nursed a forlorn hope that I might see my mother picking mushrooms on the grassy bank but the area beyond the trees was quite deserted. I glanced along the line noting that, like me, Finch held a pistol, whereas Coggins and Fowler carried cutlasses, probably reasoning that any fighting would be at close quarters. Nolan with the blunderbuss looked ready for any eventuality. I signalled to them to remain back in the tree line and went forward alone.

With my heart pounding in my chest, I hid the firearm in my pocket and yanked at the bell pull. After much drawing of bolts the door was opened and once again I was face to face with the cadaverous Mandrake.

'Ah, Major Neville,' he said. 'I regret this is

not a convenient time. Would you care to come back later?'

The man was being polite so I responded in a like manner. 'Good afternoon, Mandrake,' I said. 'Would you kindly inform Lady Neville that I am here to take her home.'

His face was as inscrutable as ever. 'Lady Neville is otherwise engaged, sir.'

I brought the pistol out of my pocket. 'I don't like having to repeat myself, Mandrake,' I said menacingly, through clenched teeth. 'Go and tell my mother I am here to take her home.'

His eyes boggled at the sight of the weapon but with an effort he managed to maintain his dignity and replied, 'Yes, sir. I will go and ascertain her availability.'

'Just go and fetch her.' I ordered.

He vanished into the house and as I turned to wave my companions forward there was a sudden commotion back in the trees. There was a frightened snort from a horse followed by muffled cries.

I heard Coggins shouted, 'Oh, no you don't, chummy,' and Sergeant finch's authoritative voice commanding, 'Stand still, or I'll shoot!'

Then all went quiet.

I ran back to the trees and found Coggins holding a figure shrouded in a long cloak under one arm. He looked very pleased with himself. The rest of my small force was grouped around him. A saddled horse, its reins trailing, stood pawing at the ground a short distance away.

Coggins gave me one of his lop-sided grins. 'We caught this one coming up behind us, Major.'

'Dan dragged him off his horse and wrapped him up in his own cloak, neat eh?' Fowler added.

'Let him go,' I said.

Finch looked puzzled. 'Let him go, sir?'

'Yes, let him go. I'm surprised you didn't recognise a horse from your own stable, Sergeant Finch.'

The big scar-faced soldier released his grip on his captive who dropped to his knees. As he did, the cloak slipped from his head.

'Would you look at that now,' Nolan whispered.

I stepped forward and helped Tobias to his feet.

'I thought I could help,' he said, brushing some dead leaves from his breeches. 'What's the situation?'

'A servant has gone to get my mother,' I replied. 'I must get back to the door.'

'Hang on, I'll come with you.' He turned to Sergeant Finch. 'I'm sorry. I should have known better than to come up behind you like that. I never was any good at playing soldiers. When I was a boy I much preferred playing shop.'

There seemed no point in a stealthy approach now. 'We'll all go,' I said. 'Fowler! Give Master Bloom your pistol.'

The young Jewish merchant held up his hands in horror at the suggestion. 'No, I couldn't carry a weapon, old boy. I wouldn't know how to use it if I did.'

* * *

The door was open, just as I'd left it. There was still no sign of Mandrake so, with the others following, I made my way cautiously along the passageway. I could hear the sound of voices and eventually found Mandrake standing before a pair of large double doors talking to a man dressed in a monk's habit. On hearing our footsteps, he turned around.

'Lady Neville is at her devotions,' he said.

I nodded towards the doors. 'Is she in there?'

The robed figure spoke. 'I forbid you to go in,' he said. It was Rushford.

Coggins stepped forward and stood towering over the dandy. 'Shall I, Major?' he asked.

'Be my guest, Coggins.'

The big man took Rushford by the scruff of his neck and shook him as a dog would shake a rat before dumping him in a corner like a bundle of old clothes. Mandrake cowered back. I stepped past him and threw open the doors.

I entered a large chamber, and immediately my nostrils were filled with the sharp, acrid smell of incense. Tall, stained-glass windows lined the walls but their intricate patterning admitted very little light, casting the room into a sombre gloominess. Two large candles burned on the high altar and yes, they were black, as Megan had said they would be. And there was something odd about the crucifix too, although at first I couldn't put my finger on it, then I realised it was upside-down.

Painted on the floor before the altar was a large five-pointed star with strange characters and writing around it that I could not decipher and standing in its centre was Edwin Cruikshank. He wore a monk's garb, as did a score or so of men who were gathered in a circle around him. I recognised the young Marquess of Bexton and several other members of the local aristocracy. There were women there also only they were not wearing the hooded robes of a religious order; in fact they were hardly wearing anything at all. All had painted faces and one of them, the one standing within the pentagram with the rogue priest, was my mother.

I got a shock when I saw Cruikshank. He looked desperately ill. His dark-rimmed eyes were sunk deep into his face, which was pallid and drawn, giving it the appearance of a death's head. A persistent cough racked his frame and he was using my mother as a support to stand upright.

'Not another step, gentlemen,' he said. 'Lest your unclean presence violate the inner sanctum.'

'I say we throw them out!' someone shouted. A chorus of agreement immediately followed and the robed assembly began to move forward aggressively.

Nolan stepped in front of me, the blunderbuss aimed at the men. 'Stay where you are!' he ordered. 'This may not be the most accurate of weapons but at this range it would surely kill some of you and make a terrible mess of the rest.'

The prospect of being blasted by a pound of buckshot had the desired effect. The Bucks' Club retreated, its members vying with each other for a position at the rear of their number.

'I must warn you,' Cruikshank shouted. 'That you risk your immortal soul if you enter the pentacle.'

'Damn you and your mumbo-jumbo,' I called back with a boldness I didn't feel.

'I wouldn't risk it, soldier-boy,' a soft voice said in my ear. It was Megan.

'How the . . . ' I began.

'Never mind that. I'm a working girl, aren't I?' She gripped my arm. 'Now, don't go rushing in there to get your mother. If you want to save yourself from all sorts of grief you must get him to send her out. Believe me, I know.'

Edwin Cruikshank was suddenly incapacitated by a violent bout of coughing. It was now or never, I thought, and I dashed forward and grabbed hold of my mother but he clung on to her and a terrible game of tug-of-war began within the pentacle. Eventually, rather than be dragged out of the five-pointed star he released his hold and fell panting on the floor. My mother swooned away and I had to carry her to the nearest pew where, with the help of Megan Griffith, I laid her down, but in doing so I turned my back on the evil priest. Hari Lal suddenly flashed into my mind with his warning to 'beware the blade'. I spun round. Cruikshank had pulled up the sleeve of his robe to reveal a wicked looking throwing knife strapped to the inside of his forearm. There was a flash of steel and the blade was in his hand and a look of triumph in his eyes.

Tobias leapt forward and caught hold of his wrist. They struggled briefly but before the young Jew could disarm him, Cruikshank turned the knife on himself, the tip of its blade piercing the rough material of his robe just beneath his rib cage. He then clamped his other hand over Tobias's and with a cry of, 'DO WHAT YOU WILL,' he drove the blade up into his own heart.

For a long moment there was a deathly hush, then a woman screamed. Nolan lowered the blunderbuss and with the threat of sudden death removed the crowd became animated, the men talking among themselves and the painted ladies squawking to be taken home. Tobias knelt by the body, his shirtfront soaked in blood. I went over to him and placed my hand on his shoulder. He looked up.

'What could possibly possess a man to do such a terrible thing?' he said quietly.

'What indeed?' I answered.

★ ★ ★

My mother was now sitting up in the pew but she was still totally oblivious to what was going on around her. Megan helped me get her to her feet and take her outside to where

Sergeant Finch had brought up the estate wagon.

Anger and frustration caused me to speak my thoughts aloud. 'How can I get her out of this damned trance!' I said.

Megan smiled. 'She'll be all right, soldier-boy. Just don't give her any more elderflower cordial.'

I said I couldn't believe a drink made from the blossom of a bush could have such a powerful effect. She turned her big hypnotic eyes on me and I experienced that strange tingling sensation that is usually described as someone walking on your grave.

'Don't underestimate my cordial, soldier-boy,' she whispered. 'The elderflowers only give it fragrance, it's the poppy heads that give it its clout.'

Then, with a delicious chuckle she ran off into the trees.

★ ★ ★

Tobias had no difficulty retrieving his horse and we set off back to Dunmere Hall. I travelled in the back of the wagon holding my mother in my arms. Coggins and Fowler just managed to squeeze in with us while Nolan rode proudly up on the box with Finch. The two men seemed to have a lot to say to each other but their voices were lost to me in the rumble of the wheels.

Hagar ran to meet us when we rattled into the cobblestone courtyard. Norbury and Smallwood, with a token force of footmen and housemaids, were waiting by the hall porch. I called them forward and gave instructions for my mother to be taken to her room and that one of the housemaids should be assigned to look after her. I then enquired after the whereabouts of my brother and my father.

I was still not used to Smallwood being the butler and it was something of a surprise when it was he who answered.

'I believe Sir Rupert and Master Giles are in the parlour, sir,' he said. 'I took the liberty of preparing a buffet luncheon.'

I was about to go into the house to break the news of Cruikshank's death when Nolan stepped forward.

'If I might have a word, sir?'

I told him to be quick.

'What I have to say won't take long, sir,' he said. He cleared his throat. 'Now that Sir Rupert is cured of his, er, affliction and is back home in the bosom of his family as it were . . . '

'Forget the blarney and get on with it, Nolan.'

'Yes, sir. Well, sir, I was thinking that the colonel would be expecting me back at the barracks . . . '

That stopped me in my tracks. My mind had been so full of thoughts of my family and of Emily that my regimental responsibilities had taken a bit of a back seat. My uncle had given me leave of absence to sort out the family estate, and having played a major part in that himself he knew I was well on the way to achieving that goal. With his brother restored to health and presumably able to take up the reins again it was logical to assume he would be expecting me to report back also.

I didn't know it at the time, but I then made a decision that was to drastically affect my future life. I had the means to mount an expedition to find Emily and now I'd more or less sorted things out at home I knew that was what I had to do.

Nolan hadn't finished. He held his hat clutched to his chest, his fingers playing nervously with the brim.

'I'm given to understand, sir,' he said, 'that there is a vacancy on the staff for a valet — for yourself, sir — and I would like to apply for the position. I could easily look after both of you, sir, you *and* Sir Rupert.'

He stood looking at me expectantly and

knew I didn't want to be parted from this small, soft-hearted Irishman. Damn it, I liked him! He was proficient in the art of looking after a gentleman, he was intelligent, loyal, and furthermore he was a good soldier. Where would I find another servant with qualities such as these?

'I'm going back to the barracks myself, Corporal, and you will come with me.'

He jumped to attention. 'Yes, sir!' he shouted.

'I've decided to resign my commission. No doubt the colonel will allow me to purchase your discharge also.'

His eyes lit up and a wide smile spread across his round face. Had it not been for years of army discipline I swear he would have danced a jig.

'And whilst I'm sure my father will be pleased to have your services it will be only a temporary arrangement as I plan to take a trip — and a gentleman's valet always accompanies him on his travels.'

Tobias arrived from the stables and we entered the house together. He seemed rather disturbed, which, I suppose, was understandable in the circumstances.

'D'you know, Thomas. I can't get Cruikshank out of my mind,' he said.

'That's hardly surprising.'

'I know, but one moment I'm sharing your dislike for him and the next I find myself empathizing with the fellow.'

'You're too compassionate, chum. You only see the good in people.'

Tobias wouldn't let it go. 'I try telling myself that he was a bad lot and the world's a better place without him but there's another voice in my head pointing out the finer things he's done.'

'Such as?'

'Helping your father when he needed money?'

'Helping him on the road to ruin, more like.'

'It was your father's greed that did that, Thomas.'

'Well, what about his drinking, then?'

He smiled condescendingly. 'Nobody forced your father to drink,' he said.

I clenched my fists in a fit of rage. 'He seduced my mother!' I hissed through my teeth.

Tobias put his arm around my shoulder. 'He brought a little romance back into her life. He made her a carefree, light-hearted girl again. She was happy, Thomas. You can't deny that.'

I shook him off. 'Listen to yourself, will you? You're defending the man who almost destroyed my family.'

He put his hands up to his head and looked at me with frightened eyes. 'You're right, Thomas. I'm sorry. What the devil's the matter with me?'

Now it was my turn to be comforting. 'Forget it. You've had one hell of a shock. You'd better get upstairs and change that shirt.'

We reached the foot of the stairs and he stopped.

'He was surprisingly sensitive and tender,' he said.

'Who, Cruikshank? You've got to be joking!'

'No, really. You were too busy caring for your mother, you didn't see.'

'See what?'

'As he lay dying he whispered something. I couldn't hear him so bent closer, and guess what he did?'

'Tell me.'

'He grabbed hold of me and pulled me down to him, in a sort of a hug — that's how I got all this blood on me — and all the time he was whispering, urgently, as though he had to finish saying whatever it was while he still had the breath to do so. I tried to make out what it was but I couldn't. If it was a foreign language it was one I'd never heard before. Anyway, he held me there and kept up his frantic gibberish until all the breath in him had gone.'

14

My father sat alone at the big round table in the parlour. He was sipping something, which, from its smell I knew to be coffee. I didn't care for the beverage myself although the coffee-houses that had sprung up in most of the larger cities were very popular, indeed they were where most of the trading took place these days and where I had tracked down a lot of my father's creditors. I was sorry my mother wasn't there with him as I'd planned, but I contented myself with the thought that she was at least safe upstairs in her own room.

Giles was standing with his back to the big window. He held a dish in his hand and was staring into it as if he expected something to surface.

'I know about Edwin,' he said. 'Megan told me.'

I was thinking that perhaps the Welsh witch could teach me a thing or two about speed-marching when he went on: 'D'you know, Tom, that woman knows me better than I know myself. I'm glad you came and took me away from St Luke's.'

He looked up at me and smiled. 'I'd have made an awful priest!'

'That was your mother's idea, Giles,' my father said. 'And a damned silly one if you ask me.'

'I now know what I really want to do with my life, father.'

'And what would that be, my boy.'

There was a look of grim determination on my brother's face when he said, 'I'm going to ask Uncle Reuben for a commission in the twenty-second.'

It seemed funny to hear Giles of all people announcing he was off to be a soldier. I was about to scoff but he stood there facing me down, daring me to rubbish the idea so I gave it some serious thought, running through a mental checklist of his attributes. I ticked off fitness and intelligence, that by nature he was light hearted and carefree and that although he thrived on adventure, given responsibility there was none who took it more seriously, which, to me, made him an ideal candidate for infantry officer training.

'It's not all fancy uniforms and jolly parties in the mess,' I said. 'A soldier's life is hard, much harder than boarding school but, if that's what you want, then go for it. I think you'll make a good officer.' I guided him out of my father's hearing. 'But you need to know that I'm going away, and I could be gone some time. I'm going to look for Emily.'

His face lit up. 'Can I come?' he asked excitedly.

'No, I'm sorry, Giles. As much as I would love to have you with me, I really need you here, at home. I'd be a lot happier knowing mother and father were in your care. I'll leave you some funds so you won't have to worry about money . . . Would you mind awfully putting off joining the Cheshire's until I get back? I'm going to see Uncle Reuben to tell him my plans so why don't you come with me? He'll be so pleased with the prospect of having you as one of his officers I'm sure he won't mind waiting.'

He shrugged his shoulders and grinned. 'Whatever you say, big brother,' he said, and then quickly becoming serious, added, 'Megan told me what it was you saved me from, so I'll do anything I can to help.'

At that moment Tobias came in. He had cleaned himself up and changed his linen but his face still had a haunted expression.

'Thomas is off to search for his lady love,' Giles said gaily.

I shot a look at father but he didn't seem to have heard, or if he had he would wait until he had me on my own before asking what was going on.

'Didn't you say she'd gone to the Carolinas?' Tobias asked.

'That's right.'

He smiled, his face lit up and I felt my friend had come back to me. 'Then you'll need passage,' he announced. 'My family know most of the skippers who sail to the Americas. We'll find you a comfortable ship with a trustworthy master . . . I take it you'll be wanting to leave from Liverpool?'

I had a sudden thought. 'Could I sail from London? It would be nice to see Clive again — and I could do with meeting your bankers.'

'*Our* bankers, old chap. They are as much yours as they are mine.' His face suddenly clouded and with uncharacteristic bitterness, he added, 'In fact yours is by far the larger account!' He then seemed to shake himself mentally and became the old Tobias again. 'Plenty of boats sail to our American colonies from the Port of London,' he said cheerfully. 'Why don't you come back with me?'

The thought of travelling in such a magnificent coach and be waited on by Hatton, Coggins and Fowler was tempting but I had things to do that would delay my departure for several days.

'I'll call on you when I get to London, if that's all right?' I said.

Norbury had put the word out that we were looking for personal servants for both my mother and my father and applicants had begun to arrive even before Tobias's coach left Dunmere Hall.

For my father, I hoped to find someone with relevant experience, and with common sense coupled with the tact of a diplomat, for my mother, a woman who not only possessed these qualities but was also tolerably proficient in hairdressing and sewing. Looking at the motley selection of hopefuls Norbury eventually ushered into the great hall, I could see I had my work cut out.

Surprisingly, finding someone for my mother was easy, as standing noticeably apart from the rest of the women was one who, although somewhat older than the others, looked both confident and capable. I called her forward and on learning that she had recently been maid to the late dowager Lady Reedsmere, I looked no further and hired her immediately.

Regrettably, none of the men stood out as she did and I was forced to go through the lengthy process of interviewing them individually. They didn't know it but they all suffered badly by comparison with Nolan and

I found myself left with only two possibles, a strikingly handsome man who, having once been a footman in Lord Vyner's household, had the required experience, and a fresh-faced, former barber's apprentice by the name of Harper, who had none. The ex-footman seemed the obvious choice but I took an instant liking to the younger man. He appeared honest and intelligent. He seemed willing to learn and eager to better his position in life, and that impressed me. Although I knew my father preferred to shave himself, I thought it no bad thing that his man should be capable of performing this task should it be required. The decision was eventually made for me when Norbury whispered that his enquiries had revealed that the former footman had been dismissed from his last place of employment for seducing almost the entire female staff.

Fortunately for me, my mother took to her new lady's maid right away and my father, rather surprisingly, seemed to enjoy sharing in the training of his new valet. So, with the problem of personal servants for my parents resolved, I felt able to leave Dunmere Hall to visit my uncle.

The day dawned sunny although cold, ideal for a brisk canter. We set of early, Giles, Nolan and me, in the sweet morning air under a cloudless, blue sky. The going was firm and we made good time, arriving at the depot in mid-afternoon. Leaving Nolan to take care of the horses, I took Giles to Uncle Reuben's office where I immediately made him aware of the reason for my visit. He crossed over to a side table without speaking and poured himself a drink. When he turned to face me his face was grim.

'I can't say this comes as a surprise,' he said sadly. 'As your CO, I'm disappointed to be losing a good company commander but as your uncle it's nothing more than I would expect from you, my boy.' He banged his glass down on the table and gathered me to him in a very un-soldierly hug. 'Damn it, Thomas, but it was good having another Neville in the mess.'

Until then, Giles had stood silent, allowing me to do all the talking. Now he spoke up. 'You can still,' he said. 'If you'll have me in the twenty-second.'

Uncle Reuben released me from his bear hug and stood with eyebrows raised regarding my tousle haired little brother. 'Are you serious?' he asked.

'Absolutely, Uncle, but you'll have to wait 'till Tom comes back from the Americas.'

'If this is the life you want, lad, I'll happily bide a year or two for you,' he said. Then, winking at me, he added, 'Give that fluffy down on your chin time to turn into a man's whiskers, eh?'

★ ★ ★

Giles and I were treated to a roisterous evening in the Officers' Mess and judging by the look of Nolan the following morning, his fellow junior NCOs had entertained him in a similar fashion. With a little help from our comrades in arms we managed to clamber into the saddle and having said our goodbyes we urged our mounts on at a gentle walk. On the journey home we told each other amusing stories and sang songs. We arrived back at Dunmere Hall in the early evening still in high spirits, but the news that awaited us there brought us back down to earth with a bump.

The stable lad, with the faithful Hagar at his heels, met us at the moat bridge and they walked with us to the hall porch where Norbury was waiting looking very grimfaced. He came up to me as I dismounted.

'I'm afraid it's your father, sir,' he announced.

My heart missed a beat. 'Has he had an accident?'

'No, sir. As far as I know he is uninjured.'

I found myself shouting. 'Then what's the matter with him!'

At the sound of my voice the others stopped what they were doing and turned to see what was going on. Norbury told the lad to take the horses up to the stables. I indicated to Nolan that he should go with him.

Once they were on their way Norbury said, 'I regret to say, sir, your father has locked himself in the wine cellar.'

'We'd better go and see,' I said, giving my brother a disapproving look as he fought to stifle a laugh.

I could hear father's strong baritone voice long before we reached the cellar steps. My father's new valet joined us en route.

'I'm really very sorry, Master Thomas,' he said. 'Sir Rupert sent me to find the steward . . . '

Norbury took up the story. 'It would seem, sir, that the master couldn't wait for Harper to return and went looking for me himself. And seeing the cellar keys on the hook in the pantry he decided to inspect the stock.'

'Sample the stock, more like,' Giles whispered.

I ignored him. 'Do you know what the master wanted with Norbury?' I asked the valet.

'I thought there must be something wrong with the brandy, sir.'

Norbury butted in. 'Harper didn't know, sir,' he said.

I rounded on the young servant. 'You gave Sir Rupert *brandy*!' I shouted.

He stepped back in alarm. 'He asked me for it, sir, after breakfast. I didn't think it would do any harm, sir. I thought it would buck him up a bit, him being a bit down this morning.'

Giles rolled his eyes at me. It was the old, old story, father's 'eye-opener' to help him cope with the day ahead leading to excess.

It was wrong of me to vent my anger on the most inexperienced member of the household staff. 'I'm sorry, Harper, you weren't to know,' I said.

The young man was visibly embarrassed to receive an apology from his employer. He looked away, fumbling in the capacious centre pocket of his apron, eventually producing a bunch of keys that wouldn't have looked out of place in the Tower of London.

'I got these from the gatehouse, sir,' he said, still avoiding eye contact. 'There are duplicates of every key in the house here.'

'Well done, lad!' Giles shouted. He snatched them from him and began trying them one by one in the lock.

The door was quickly opened and we all filed down the cellar steps, my father's voice getting louder all the time. Years had past since my last visit to the small underground chamber but it was just as I remembered it, cool but not cold and with not a trace of dampness. Perhaps the ceiling did seem a touch lower but the dusty, bottle-filled shelves around the walls looked just the same. Light was provided by several candles stuck into empty wine bottles on a small wooden table in the middle of the floor. And there, slumped in the only chair, was my father, a bottle in one hand and a glass in the other, singing his heart out. He was still singing when Harper and Nolan carried both him and the chair up to his bedroom, which is where we left him to sleep off the effects of an excess of alcohol.

My mother showed genuine concern for her husband, which I found quite touching and very gratifying. Away from Cruikshank's influence she was more her old self although she was subject to worrying bouts of melancholy. On these occasions I was thankful for the devotion and solicitude of her maid and thanked my lucky stars that this experienced and capable woman had been available to take on the job.

With reliable servants to watch over my parents (what Harper may lack in experience he more than made up for in enthusiasm and dedication) I felt that I had everything covered. There was Smallwood to run the house and Benson the estate, all under the eagle eye of the indomitable Norbury.

But for all that, it was to be a full month before I felt sufficiently comfortable with my parent's condition to hand the reins over to Giles and set off for London.

15

Archie Fowler was trying to catch his breath, beside him stood a tiny street urchin; his dirty face one huge smile.

'It's no good trying to speed-march through these crowded streets, Major,' he panted. 'To get anywhere fast you have to be a dodger like this little rascal. It took me all my time to keep up with him.'

★ ★ ★

Throughout the coach journey from the north a small man with a loud voice had talked endlessly and with great enthusiasm about the expansion of the capital. He spoke of a new middle-class whose purpose-built dwellings were creeping relentlessly westward and engulfing the surrounding villages. Nowhere, he said, was this more evident than in the rapidly expanding borough of St Marylebone, which we were now driving through.

Our self-appointed guide announced that we would soon be arriving at our destination so I began looking for someone I could send to the Clive's house in Queen Square.

As we rumbled into the courtyard of the coaching inn I spotted a likely candidate, and almost before the heavy vehicle had stopped rocking on its springs, I leapt out and grabbed him. I told him I'd reward him handsomely if he were to return with written confirmation that he had delivered my message. The lad did better than that; he returned with Archie Fowler.

On this occasion the chirpy Cockney was not wearing Clive's ostentatious scarlet and gold livery but a shabby, brown coat that looked rather incongruous over his silk breeches and hose. He looked full of concern.

'The house is shut up, sir. The master has gone off electioneering and the mistress has gone with him.'

This was a disappointment as I had been looking forward to seeing my friend and mentor again.

'It can't be helped,' I said, philosophically. 'But I do need to see Master Bloom. Can you take me to his house?'

Fowler's little ferret-like face lit up. 'No problem, sir. The sergeant major's been there lots of times. He'll show you the way.'

'Isn't Hatton with his master?'

'Gawd love you, no, sir,' he grinned. 'The master's cousin, Sir Edward, sent his carriage to take the General and his lady down to Cornwall . . . Bill Hatton will be only too pleased to have something to do — In fact, we all would.'

If we were to stay at the inn tonight I wasn't going to have Nolan roughing it with the other servants so I booked us two adjoining rooms on the same balcony. Then, after depositing our baggage and refreshing ourselves with a swift tankard of ale apiece, we followed Fowler out onto the streets of London.

I was impressed by the modern, terrace style of building, which I thought neat and orderly. This seemed to be reflected in the passers-by who looked on the whole to be well behaved and mannerly. I mentioned this to my tame Londoner, Archie Fowler.

'Yeah, nice round here, innit?' he said, giving me a wicked grin. 'But just down there is Regent Street which is a den of thieves and cutthroats — don't go there without a weapon. And over in the other direction is Holborn, where I come from — don't go there, even if you have got a weapon.'

He laughed at this but I noticed Nolan drop a discreet pace behind me and walk with a hand in the pocket of his coat where I guessed he carried his pistol.

Queen Square was not far, so it wasn't long

before we found ourselves at Robert Clive's London house. Fowler took us down some steps to a basement kitchen where a large range filled the whole of one wall and rows of copper pots on shelves another. A huge wooden table stood in the centre of the floor with a few chairs dotted around.

'I'm sorry to have to bring you down here, sir,' he said. 'But, as I told you, the house is shut up. There's covers over everything upstairs.'

I wrinkled my nose. 'I take it Cook's been given a holiday as well?' I said.

'Yes, along with the scullery maid.' He raised an eyebrow. 'But how did you know that?'

'Tobacco smoke. I don't think you'd be smoking in the kitchen if Cook were here.'

'There's only Dan and me in the house — we didn't have nowhere else to go — and Bill Hatton, of course, who stayed on to look after the horses . . . I'll go and fetch him.'

The former company sergeant major strode into the kitchen grinning from ear to ear closely followed by big Daniel Coggins, the familiar leer on his round, scarred face. Archie Fowler brought up the rear. When the three men were within a yard of me they stopped and stood in line and, as one man, came to attention. Some may think this strange but I did not. I knew these grizzled, battle-scarred veterans were paying me a far greater compliment than any hand-pumping or backslapping could ever be.

'At ease, gentlemen,' I said, smiling.

Hatton spoke. 'You want me to take you to Master Bloom's house, sir?'

'I'd be grateful.'

'You wait here then, sir, and I'll bring the *Phaeton* round. Give me a hand, will you, Dan?'

They left, and once again there were just the three of us in the kitchen. For a fleeting moment Fowler looked uncomfortable. Then his face lit up.

'Would you like some ale, sir — Barney?'

We both agreed and he relaxed visibly. Crossing to the table he poured us a tankard apiece, and one for himself.

'You mentioned earlier you would all be pleased to have something to do,' I said. 'Is that because the Clives are away?'

He took a gulp from his pot before answering. 'There's only the horses to look after and the sergeant major does that. There's nothing for Dan and me to do.'

'You're kept busy when the family are at home?'

'Nah! The general and his wife 'as got their own servants. He brought 'em over from India.'

'I assumed you were employed as footmen.'

He chuckled at that. 'Can you see us waiting at table? One look at old Dan's ugly mug and you'd be put off your grub for good!'

This set me thinking but before I could put my thoughts into words Coggins' round face appeared at the door to tell me Hatton was outside with the *Phaeton*.

They were an ill-matched pair, but good to have around. 'How would the two of you like to come with me to America?'

They looked at each other for a moment and Fowler spoke. 'The general won't mind. I reckon he only gave us a job 'cos we was out of work.' The cheeky grin was back to his face. 'If it's all right with the sergeant major, it's all right with us. What d'you say, Dan?'

The big man nodded enthusiastically.

★ ★ ★

The route to the Bloom's house took us very near the Thames, the low tide mud adding a certain piquancy to the all-pervading smell of horse droppings. I held my silk kerchief to my nose as Hatton drove though dirty, narrow streets, eventually stopping the small carriage at a tall, three-storey building, the largest in a row of Dutch-style houses

292

backing onto the river.

'Here we are, Major,' he announced. 'I'll stay with the horse, if that's all right with you?'

I told him about my plans to sail to the Carolinas. He wasn't surprised.

'I know, sir. Fowler told me,' he said. 'I only wish I could come with you but I have responsibilities here.' I guessed he was making it easy for me. 'And I'm not as young as I used to be,' he added with a smile.

He was right, of course. As much as I would have liked to have him with me, and Finch too for that matter, their days of derring-do were well and truly behind them. The eager Irishman and the two former Company soldiers would be my only companions on the forthcoming expedition.

I entered the building, closely followed by Nolan. It was gloomy inside but very quickly I made out a row of high desks, at which a number of clerks were busily working.

'Can I help you gentlemen?'

The speaker was an elderly man who, like his fellows, was dressed all in black with a white clerical collar.

'I wish to see Master Bloom.'

The greybeard looked me up and down before replying: 'Would that be Master Isaac or Master Samuel, sir,' he said snootily.

'Neither. The Bloom I seek is called Tobias.'

At the mention of the name, the man lost his haughtiness and looked around desperately for assistance. Help arrived in the form of a tall, lean man whose slight stoop and a veritable eagle's beak of a nose gave him an almost bird-like appearance. He introduced himself as Tobias's uncle, Isaac. I told him who I was and that Tobias had offered to arrange a passage for me to the Carolinas.

He weighed me up, a condescending smile on his face. I smiled back, smug in the knowledge that he had probably seen me arrive in the very latest *Phaeton* driven by a liveried driver.

'The *Caprice* sails for Charleston in two days time, Major. I would be happy to arrange a berth for you — and accommodation in the fo'c'sle for your man, of course.'

'I shall require four berths,' I said. 'I'll not have my servants roughing it with the seamen.'

He rubbed his hands together at the thought of such a lucrative order. 'Of course, sir,' he beamed. 'Will you be paying cash?'

'I will give you a note you can present at the bank . . . Now, if can I see Tobias?'

He looked uncomfortable. 'I regret to say that my nephew has had a seizure, sir. He is confined to his bed.'

The news came as a shock and for a moment I couldn't think straight. 'I would still like to see him,' I said at length. 'He is my friend. We were in India together.'

Isaac instructed the elderly clerk to despatch one of his minions to inform his nephew I was here. He then guided me to what was obviously the boardroom and sat me at a huge mahogany table, placing before me a pen and paper and a large glass of sherry. He would have taken Nolan away, presumably to the servant's quarters, but I insisted that he remain with me. Several glasses of sherry later, (which Nolan, not having been offered anything other than water, helped me to dispose of) Isaac led me up three flights of stairs to Tobias's quarters.

This proved to be a large, airy room with the sound of the dockside bustle many feet below wafting in through the tall french windows, which, in spite of a chill wind, stood open wide. Fresh air and plenty of it seems to have taken over from leeches as the cure-all these days and it wouldn't have surprised me to find Tobias actually on the balcony outside. As it was, he lay propped up in a big, brass bed looking absolutely awful. His face was gaunt and there was a grotesque droop to the left-hand corner of his mouth. His hair, which I was surprised to see was streaked with grey, clung limp and damp-looking across his brow.

'He was found lying on the ground at the door of the synagogue,' Isaac whispered. 'He is completely paralysed down one side but apart from that he seems to be in good health.'

'Thank you, uncle — and you, Nolan, if you please,' the patient said, dismissively. 'I'd like to be left alone with Major Neville.' He slurred his words like a drunkard but his eyes were bright and alert.

As soon as we were alone, I said, 'I am so sorry to find you like this, Tobias.'

'So am I, old boy,' he replied with a twisted grin. He struggled to sit up in his bed, his expression serious, his eyes wide and beseeching.

'I keep getting the most weird ideas in my head, Thomas. Thoughts that I wouldn't normally give the time of day seem to sit there and grow. I have become a misanthrope, a cynic who can no longer see any good in people — and I find myself longing to indulge in fantasises that a gentleman shouldn't even think about.'

I was searching for something to say when he suddenly winced as if gripped by a sharp pain. The spasm passed quickly but left him lying sweating and breathless on his pillow. I mopped his brow with my kerchief.

'D'you remember when we talked about a demon or an evil spirit taking possession of someone?' he whispered.

I nodded, wondering what was coming next.

'At the time I thought it was all a lot of nonsense but the other day, when I tried to enter the synagogue I couldn't. No matter how hard I tried, Thomas, I just couldn't do it. It was as though I was fighting with myself. I made one supreme effort — and this is the result.'

He took hold of my arm with his one good hand, gripping it tightly, his eyes locked onto mine. I could see beads of sweat forming on his brow.

'They say in the scriptures that when someone is out of their mind, they are possessed. I've always put that down to superstition, a lack of medical knowledge in the olden days — but now I'm not so sure. We all have a dark side, which, in the normal course of events, we manage to keep under control, but mine seems set on taking over. I'm afraid to go to sleep at night, Thomas. I fear I haven't the strength to fight this thing much longer.'

Isaac came back to plead that his nephew

needed rest, so I took my leave. Tobias returned my see-you-soon grin with a lopsided smile. At the door I looked back. The mask had slipped. In his eyes there was an almost fanatical gleam, which at first I took to be fear — but knowing Tobias, it could just as well have been some sort of gritty determination.

I spent the whole of the following day at the inn, sending and receiving messengers. One of Bloom's clerks arrived with confirmation that berths had been booked for my party on the *Caprice*. A liveried courier brought me letters of credit from my bank and Nolan was despatched to Clive's house with instructions for Coggins and Fowler, telling them when and where to report and what to bring with them.

My old regimental sergeant, the one with the American colonial experience, had taken great delight in regaling new recruits with lurid accounts of the hostile natives in that part of the world, so I made sure that my baggage included plenty of powder and shot. He had also spoken of the settlers clothing being made of deer hide, which, I remember thinking at the time, must be rather smelly and uncomfortable to wear. The people at the inn knew of no tailor in the vicinity specialising in such attire so I decided that if, when we got to Charleston, garments made from animal skin were felt to be necessary, we would kit ourselves out there.

★ ★ ★

The big day duly arrived, and Hatton drove Nolan and me to the docks in Clive's big coach with Fowler and Coggins standing on the box at the back looking very pleased with themselves.

The Pool of London was a sea of masts, the quayside a noisy scene of dockworkers loading and unloading both vessels moored there and the lighters that shuttled to and fro between the docks and the ships anchored in the river. In his clerical garb, Isaac Bloom stood out from the roughly dressed labourers that milled about him like a magpie among a flock of sparrows. Hatton skilfully steered his horses around a group busily stacking barrels before bringing them to a halt opposite the tall, beaky merchant.

He stood by a gangplank leading up to the deck of a two-masted square-rigger. The ship looked clean and well cared for, which spoke well of her master.

Tobias was uppermost in my thoughts. I alighted quickly from the carriage and asked how he was.

Isaac shook his head sadly. 'He is much the same, Major. The doctor says he desperately needs rest but he doesn't listen.'

A bearded man wearing a rough calico shirt and canvas trousers ran down from the ship. He touched a knuckle to his forehead and, addressing Isaac, who, I suppose, looked the most imposing member of our little group, asked us to board without delay.

'Skipper says if we don't get underway now we'll miss the tide,' he explained.

Hatton solemnly shook hands with each of us in turn. He didn't speak but his eyes were flooded with tears and I doubt if he could have spoken if he'd tried.

The sailor helped Nolan with my cabin trunk and Fowler and Coggins carried the rest of the luggage between them. I was about to say goodbye to Isaac when he surprised me by walking up the gangplank before me.

Waiting for us on deck was a tall, fair-haired man with a neatly trimmed, moustache-less beard and piercing blue eyes. After greeting the merchant he held a big hand out to me.

'You will be Major Neville,' he said with a disarming smile. 'I am Captain Jensen. Welcome aboard, sir. My steward will show you to your quarters.'

He snapped his fingers at a stoutish man

with heavy jowls who, for all his fleshiness, looked as though he could hold his own among the fo'c'sle hands.

Orders were shouted and there was a sudden bustle of activity. Men ran to the capstan, the gangplank was pulled up, ropes were cast off and sails billowed out with a crack.

Seeing my puzzled look, Isaac quickly explained that the ship was in the hands of a Thames pilot. 'I'll go back with him when he's rowed ashore,' he said.

The portly steward showed us to our quarters. We were all accommodated in the stern. I had a small cabin with two bunks; the others shared a cabin designed for four. It would seem that we were the only passengers. It was all very satisfactory.

Out on deck there was still a great deal going on. The city, with its skyline of beautiful church spires, was behind us and we were heading into the country. Barges passed us, low in the water with heavy cargo. Their big red sails flapped impotently as our tall vessel stole their wind.

The river widened and there were more shouted commands from the quarterdeck. Our canvas was reduced and we slowed down appreciably. The order was then given to drop anchor and we came to rest.

A small boat put out from the shore and rowed steadily towards us. There was one man at the oars and another sat wrapped in a cape in the stern. The Thames pilot said his goodbyes and made his way to the rail where Isaac Bloom joined him. It didn't take long for the boat to reach us. The pilot shouted something and a couple of sailors appeared with a scrambling net, which they dropped over the side. Isaac seemed agitated. He called down to the boat and shortly after the man in the cape appeared at the rail and climbed aboard.

He looked familiar. Then I remembered where I'd seen him before. He was the clerk Isaac had sent to the Inn to confirm my passage. What the man had to say was obviously urgent and serious. He spoke in low tones but with a great deal of gesturing. As Isaac listened he wrung his hands, the pilot stood to one side looking decidedly uncomfortable. I went over to find out what was going on. The old merchant saw me coming and turned towards me, his face a mask of grief.

'Tobias is dead.'

I must have faltered because I found the pilot supporting me, his hand on my elbow. The news shouldn't have come as a surprise. Tobias had told me himself he didn't have the strength to carry on but death is so final and always difficult to accept.

'His heart gave out?' I suggested.

'No, sir.' It was the messenger. 'He leapt from his balcony.'

Isaac looked heavenwards saying something about mortal sin, the messenger dug deep into his cloak and brought out a small parcel tied with string.

'This was on his bed. It's addressed to you, Major,' he said.

I undid the string and unfolded the paper carefully. Tears burned my eyes, for wrapped in my silk kerchief was Tobias's gold fob watch.

Author's note.

The Newab of Bengal, the sadistic, Suraja Dowla, a firm supporter of the French, captured the British garrison at Fort William and imprisoned 156 men and women in a small cell, twenty feet square, where all but 23 suffocated during the night. This was to become infamously known as the 'Black Hole of Calcutta'.

Robert Clive, who had returned to India as governor of Fort David, was immediately despatched to Bengal where, at Plassey, on the 23rd June 1757, with a mostly native force of just over 3,000 men, he defeated the Newab's army of over 50,000.

Suraja Dowla was deposed, and the pro-British prince, Mir Jafar, was installed as Newab in his place. Clive was made Governor of Bengal and created Baron Clive of Plassey by a grateful government.

He was also made very rich by a grateful Mir Jafa.

Later, when called before a parliamentary committee to answer for the huge private fortune he had amassed in India, he gave his famous reply:

'Gentlemen, I stand astonished at my own moderation.'

★   ★   ★

And Thomas Neville sailed to the Carolinas to find his sweetheart, but that's another story.

We do hope that you have enjoyed reading this large print book.

Did you know that all of our titles are available for purchase?

We publish a wide range of high quality large print books including:
Romances, Mysteries, Classics
General Fiction
Non Fiction and Westerns

Special interest titles available in large print are:
The Little Oxford Dictionary
Music Book
Song Book
Hymn Book
Service Book

Also available from us courtesy of Oxford University Press:
Young Readers' Dictionary
(large print edition)
Young Readers' Thesaurus
(large print edition)

For further information or a free brochure, please contact us at:
Ulverscroft Large Print Books Ltd.,
The Green, Bradgate Road, Anstey,
Leicester, LE7 7FU, England.
Tel: (00 44) 0116 236 4325
Fax: (00 44) 0116 234 0205

Other titles published by
The House of Ulverscroft:

THE FINAL CURTAIN

Ken Holdsworth

With shoulder-length blond hair and cornflower-blue eyes, Ronnie Simmons is quite irresistible to his fellow actors — of both sexes — and in the jaundiced opinion of his boyhood friend, TV soap actor Nick Carter, he loses his heart with regularity. So it is surprising when Ronnie's sister, Susan, begs him to talk her brother out of his latest relationship. Being between jobs, Nick sets out for the rural backwater where Ronnie is appearing with an Arts Council sponsored touring company — but behind the idyllic pastoral facade lies a disturbing mystery, and Nick is soon involved in violence and murder . . .

THE CONDOR'S FEATHER

Margaret Muir

Forsaking the demands of nineteenth century society and Huntingley's luxuries, Thia Beresford decides to embark on a riding expedition across the pampas of Patagonia. Thia joins the ship in Liverpool, accompanied by her father, brother, a playwright, two servants and her Newfoundland dogs. Welshman Euan Davies acts as their guide when they disembark in South America. But soon Davies's disturbing secret unravels and Thia's party becomes embroiled in a deadly game of cat and mouse with a group of dangerous prison escapees. Beset by Indians, inhospitable terrain, pampas winds and mountain lions, how can this mismatched group of travellers survive?

LORD LUCAN: MY STORY

William Coles

The Lord Lucan Scandal is one of the greatest and most extraordinary mysteries of the twentieth-century. Ever since Lucky Lord Lucan disappeared in 1974 after the murder of his nanny, the world has wondered what happened to Britain's most dashing Peer. Here, in his own hand, is the answer. This is Lord Lucan's personal memoir of his life as the world's most infamous fugitive. It is the story of an Old Etonian Earl on the run; of how a man became a murderer; and how a life-long friendship soured into an enduring hate. Here, and for the first time, is the full monstrous account of the life of Lord Lucan. This is his story.

THE RYBINSK DECEPTION

Colin D. Peel

When the crew of a Russian supertanker is found dying of radiation poisoning, four people's futures hang in the balance . . . David Coburn: working undercover at the remote outpost he's infiltrated. Hari Tan: modern-day pirate operating in the Malacca Strait. Heather Cameron: UNICEF nurse helping exploited children on a beach of toxic waste. Luther O'Halloran: nuclear defence analyst on assignment to the US National Counter-Proliferation Centre . . . There is a conspiracy so menacing that Coburn must halt an attack on a warship in the Yellow Sea, or the US will enter into conflict with an enemy whose nuclear capability is frighteningly real . . .

BLOOD AND SANGRIA

Robert Charles

Detective Sergeant Judy Kane resigned from the Breckland Police and joined her husband Ben to run a harbour-front bar in Porto Viejo in Spain. Judy's crime fighting instincts are roused when a body is trawled up from the sea in the nets of a fishing boat, and she discovers that the victim was one of her old training friends. Someone is running a joint piracy and drug smuggling operation: yachts are disappearing; their owners murdered and thrown overboard. The two prime suspects are both named Harry — which one is it? . . . Judy and Ben's lives depend upon getting the answer right.

SURVIVORS

Terry Nation

Flight 301 from Paris to London disembarks seven minutes late after a passenger is taken ill on board. Within weeks, the killer disease he was carrying has wiped out most of the world's population. Power, water and food supplies fail, cities become open graves and nature lays waste to civilisation. The survivors must start again in a post-apocalyptic world: Abby is searching for her son; Jenny flees from London; she encounters Greg, an engineer, and they form a community. But they face terrible dangers — not just the trials of day-to-day life, but also the deadly threat from other survivors . . .